THE DEAD ZONE

Carrying a flashlight, Mark Stevens led the Hardys out into his backyard. He turned the light on, shining it over a rose garden.

Joe touched one of the drooping dark red roses. Its petals fell under his touch. "It's dead," he said.

Stevens nodded. "That's happening to all my flowers. The gardener can't explain it." His voice dropped. "I don't know if I can finish my manuscript. Too much of it is coming true!"

"Has there been anything else?" Frank asked.

"There's this." Stevens turned the flashlight's beam toward another flower bed. The light played over a tombstone that had been set among the dead flowers.

A gargoyle's head was perched on top of the stone, and words were carved into its granite surface. "Stevens," it read. "Rest in peace."

"Look at the date of death," Stevens said in a trembling voice. "It's two weeks from today!"

Books in THE HARDY BOYS CASEFILES® Series

Available from ARCHWAY Paperbacks

THE HARDY BOYS CASEFILES No. 71

REAL HORROR

FRANKLIN W. DIXON

AN ARCHWAY PAPERBACK
Published by POCKET BOOKS

New York   London   Toronto   Sydney   Tokyo   Singapore

This book is a work of fiction. Names, characters, places, and incidents are either the product of the author's imagination or are used fictitiously. Any resemblance to actual events or locales or persons, living or dead, is entirely coincidental.

AN ARCHWAY PAPERBACK *Original*

An Archway Paperback published by
POCKET BOOKS, a division of Simon & Schuster Inc.
1230 Avenue of the Americas, New York, NY 10020

Copyright © 1993 by Simon & Schuster Inc.
Produced by Mega-Books of New York, Inc.

ISBN: 0-671-73107-6

First Archway Paperback printing January 1993

10 9 8 7 6 5 4 3 2 1

THE HARDY BOYS, AN ARCHWAY PAPERBACK and colophon are registered trademarks of Simon & Schuster Inc.

THE HARDY BOYS CASEFILES is a trademark of Simon & Schuster Inc.

Cover art by Brian Kotzky

Printed in the U.S.A.

IL 6+

Chapter

1

"MURDER IS MY BUSINESS," said the heavyset man sitting onstage. "Violence and gore are the tools of my trade. No one believes in vampires or werewolves anymore, so today's monsters are usually human."

He grinned, his teeth gleaming as a white crescent against his jet black beard. "Today's audience still wants real horror, but of a human kind."

Seated in the front row of the auditorium, eighteen-year-old Frank Hardy was surprised that he was enjoying himself. He hadn't been thrilled about spending his afternoon inside a crowded theater. Who wanted to waste a beautiful late-summer day listening to a novelist talk about horror writing? Frank had to admit, though, that the guy was pretty entertaining.

Brushing back his brown hair, Frank leaned in toward his brother. "Not bad," he whispered to Joe. "I'm glad you talked me into coming."

"You should listen to me more often," Joe said, unable to keep the slight smirk off his face. A year younger than Frank, Joe had the blond good looks and solid muscular build of an athlete. Frank was an athlete, too, but his muscles were long and lean, like those of a swimmer or tennis player. Both boys liked fast-paced action, and as the sons of world-famous detective Fenton Hardy, they'd seen plenty of it. Joe and Frank had earned excellent reputations as crime fighters, too.

Ordinarily, Joe would be the last person to buy a ticket for a lecture. This wasn't any ordinary lecture, though. The speaker was Mark Stevens, "Master of Modern Terror."

Joe had read every one of Stevens's books, and he couldn't pass up a chance to meet him. It had meant making a thirty-minute drive to Ashfork, an affluent little community just south of their hometown of Bayport, but it was worth it.

Mark Stevens was speaking in the Ashfork Playhouse, a grand old theater with plush seats and expensive flocked wallpaper. Joe had enjoyed watching clips of the movies that were made from Stevens's books, even though he had already seen each of them. The short story Stevens read had made Joe's skin crawl.

Joe kept his eyes focused on the stage, where

Stevens was in the middle of a question-and-answer session. The writer paused and sipped from a glass of water. Putting down the glass, he asked, "Any other questions?"

A red-haired teenager at Joe's right stuck his hand into the air. "Do you believe in the supernatural?" he asked.

"Funny you should ask." Stevens lifted a pile of papers from the small table beside him. "My new novel touches on the subject. It's about a haunting, but with a twist. It's been a very . . . challenging book to work on."

Joe saw the writer's attention wander briefly. Recovering, Stevens said, "I'm still working on it, but I'll read from one of the passages for you."

Smiling, Stevens slipped on a pair of half glasses. He leafed through the pages to find his starting point.

Holding the manuscript before him, he started in. " 'Beware the dead. Sometimes they knock on your door. . . .' "

Frank had to admit that Stevens was a captivating speaker who read with an easy flair. Most of the audience was entranced. Frank, however, found himself not paying attention.

He could hear something—some kind of noise just under Stevens's words. Cupping his ear, he focused his hearing on it.

A low moaning seemed to be building inside the playhouse.

As the noise grew louder, Stevens had to stop. He tapped the wireless microphone. "Feedback," he suggested weakly. Looking at his manuscript again, Stevens raised his voice over the noise.

It didn't help. Frank and Joe had to cover their ears as the noise increased in pitch, blotting out Stevens's words. As the pitch increased, the tone changed. It didn't sound like moaning any longer. It sounded as if someone were screaming.

Stevens had to stop reading again. Joe tapped Frank's shoulder. "Look," he said out loud.

Frank followed the direction of Joe's pointing finger.

Mounted on the rear wall of the stage were two large ceramic carvings, king-size reproductions of the twin masks of Comedy and Tragedy. Frank guessed they were about seven feet high and four feet wide. Each mask was carved to resemble a human face. The Comedy mask had a smiling mouth. The mouth of the Tragedy mask was turned down to express sadness. Both masks peered out on the audience with empty stares. Their eyes were almond-shaped hollows, and the total effect was eerie.

The masks were shaking now from the sound. They tugged against their anchors, as if being rattled by an unseen hand.

Frank shifted uneasily. These masks were

huge. If one of them broke loose and fell, Stevens could get badly hurt.

As the boys watched, tiny puffs of smoke erupted from the hollow eye sockets. Then liquid began to seep from the openings, dripping down the surface of the masks and splattering onto the stage.

The liquid was thick and red—like blood.

"Stop it!" Stevens cried, covering his ears.

All at once the screaming ended. As it did, the masks stopped rocking. They trembled slightly before lying still against the wall again. The last of the red liquid dribbled away.

"Amazing!" Frank cried out. "Talk about special effects."

Behind the Hardys, the crowd had burst into an excited buzz. Joe tried to speak with Frank, but it was impossible to hear.

"Idiots!" An angry voice cut through the clamor, silencing the audience. Frank and Joe turned, trying to find the speaker.

A middle-aged man stood at the back of the auditorium. Dressed in a faded brown wool sport jacket, he was of medium height with big bones and a strong build. His long white hair spilled to his shoulders.

"Screaming ghosts?" the man jeered. "Vibrating masks? How stupid do you think we are, Stevens?"

"Who—?" Mark Stevens shaded his eyes

from the overhead lights. "Ramsey? Deke Ramsey?"

"You know who it is." Ramsey's face was puffy and unshaven. With the aid of a wooden cane, he began walking down the center aisle to the stage. "How could you forget? You destroyed my career!"

The color drained from Stevens's face. The hand that held the microphone dropped heavily into his lap.

Frank and Joe glanced at each other.

"Trouble," Joe muttered.

"Yeah," Frank agreed. "Big time." Ramsey seemed loud and combative, and he had picked up his cane, brandishing it as if it were a weapon. Things could get very ugly, very fast, Frank thought.

Ramsey continued his march down the aisle, his cane lowered to the floor. "You've always liked publicity stunts, Stevens," he said loudly. "That's what this is, isn't it? Something to attract a little attention for the book you're writing."

"No!" Stevens insisted. "I just came here to meet my fans and give a talk on my writing."

"Liar!" Ramsey screamed.

Stevens wiped his forehead nervously. This is getting out of hand, Frank thought.

Seated at the edge of the aisle, Frank stood up as Ramsey stalked past him. Ramsey's eyes were gray, and they flashed with the vivid anger of a much younger man. Reaching out, Frank caught Ramsey's worn coat sleeve. "I think you should sit down," Frank said quietly and simply.

Joe stepped in behind his brother, ready to help.

Ramsey hesitated. "But—" His shoulders sagged in defeat. "All right," he uttered in a low voice.

Frank released his sleeve, and Ramsey started back up the aisle. Without warning he turned back, raised his cane like a baseball bat, and swung with savage fury. Frank brought up his arms to protect himself as the cane's thick brass handle whistled toward his head.

The handle smashed against his forearms, the painful blow sending Frank reeling backward.

Joe steadied him. "Are you okay?"

Frank grimaced as he watched Ramsey run toward the stage. "We've got to stop that guy. He's crazy!"

A few people behind Frank and Joe left their seats and rushed for the side exits. Somebody'll call the cops, Joe thought, but it's going to be too late. Mark Stevens needs help *now*.

Ramsey climbed the stairs onto the stage as Stevens got up and backed away from the man.

"I'm writing a new book, too," Ramsey told Stevens in a voice loud enough for the Hardys

7

to hear. "It's a story about a haunted house—just like yours. You've always used your gimmicks, your tricks, to overshadow my work. Never again!"

Joe Hardy was already running toward the steps on the left side of the stage.

Frank hurried to the right, to the other set of stairs. He didn't want to give Ramsey a chance to escape. Frank kept his eyes on the stage as he ran.

Stevens was inching back toward the rear wall. Scuttling, he stepped in a puddle of red liquid. With a loud cry, the author slipped and fell and ended up on his back, directly under the giant Tragedy mask.

Ramsey stood over him. "Revenge," he snarled, loud enough for the Hardys to hear. He raised his cane, its brass head gleaming under the lights.

"No!" Joe shouted as he ran onto the stage.

Frank climbed up the steps from the other side. "Put the cane down," he said.

Slowly Ramsey lowered his arm. "You owe me," he told Stevens as he backed away. "You know you do. You've ruined my life. One way or another, you're going to pay me back."

Ramsey crossed to the front of the stage. Without hesitating, he jumped off it onto the floor below.

Quickly he pushed his way into the exiting crowd. "I'll get him," Frank declared.

8

"Let him go," Mark Stevens called out. "Please. Catching him will only make things worse."

Standing at the edge of the stage, Frank stopped. Ramsey pushed through the front doors and out of sight into the lobby.

Joe approached Stevens. Still sitting in the pile of goo, the writer looked obviously shaken.

He took the hand Joe extended to him. "Thanks," Stevens said, pulling himself upright. "I don't know what would have happened if you two hadn't been here."

"Why didn't you want Ramsey captured?" Joe asked.

"It wouldn't do any good," Stevens replied. "The police would question him, then release him. He'd just end up hating me more."

Scccrtch. Joe's comment was cut off by the sound of squealing metal. At a single glance Joe realized what was happening.

Behind Stevens the huge ceramic Tragedy mask was pulling away from the back wall. One of its supporting hooks had broken. The mask was now dangling loose over their heads.

"Get off the stage!" Joe shouted.

Following Joe's gaze, Stevens twisted around. At the sight of the tilted mask, he jerked forward in fear. As he did, his feet slid out from under him. Before Joe could catch him, Stevens fell, sprawling flat on the stage.

Joe bent down to help him. At that exact moment he heard a sharp snap.

Joe raised his head as the huge mask broke free of its last support. Falling away from the wall, it toppled forward.

Joe and Stevens were about to be crushed!

Chapter

2

"LOOK OUT!" Frank yelled from the front edge of the stage. There was no time for him to do anything but scream. He was too far away to help.

Joe clutched at Stevens's shirt and knotted the fabric in his fists. He pushed off with his legs, throwing himself backward. Stevens was dragged along with him.

The two of them rolled away just as the mask crashed down on the stage with a deafening noise. It shattered into countless pieces in the pool of bloodlike goo.

Joe released Stevens as they came to a stop, the remains of the mask only a few feet from them.

Frank raced over to them. He saw that Stevens's face was pale, but he seemed unhurt. Joe was already getting to his feet.

Frank could hear a sudden swell of voices from the auditorium. He had been so focused on Joe that he'd forgotten that others were there, too.

"Mark!" a man's voice called out. Frank watched as a man and a woman ran up the steps and onto the stage.

The man was short and balding and dressed in an expensive-looking suit. Ignoring the Hardys, he leaned over Stevens. "You could have been killed!"

"Yes," he said. "I know that." Raising his eyes to the woman, he asked, "Joyce? What are you doing here?"

Stevens got to his feet and looked at the Hardys. "This is Joyce Halloran, publicist, and Robert Lipp, my agent." He turned to them, gesturing at Frank and Joe. "And these are my rescuers."

Joyce Halloran was a tall blond woman in her late thirties. Joe thought she seemed nervous because she was plucking at the hem of her tailored jacket. "I—I was in the back," she stammered. "For the, um, publicity stunt."

"What?" Stevens bellowed. "*You* did that? The noise, the blood capsules?"

Joyce flinched. "When the screaming started, you really seemed worried—I knew something had gone wrong then."

"It scared me half to death," Stevens said. "You should have told me you were going to do this!"

"I did," Joyce protested. "Well—I told Mr. Lipp. Weeks ago."

The balding man nodded. "I sent a note with your last batch of contracts, Mark. I bet you haven't even looked at them, have you?"

Stevens shook his head sheepishly. "No."

From outside the theater came the sound of approaching sirens. "The police," Joe said. "When they get here, they're going to have a crime to investigate."

Joe's words attracted everyone's attention. He was standing next to the wall examining the metal clasps that had held the broken mask to the wall.

"Wh-what do you mean?" Joyce asked in a tiny voice. "That mask was installed by professional stagehands just this morning."

"The metal hooks on it were hacksawed almost all the way through. Once the mask started shaking during your publicity stunt, the hooks would have to break. This was a setup so that someone would get hurt."

"Who would do such a thing?" Robert Lipp asked indignantly.

Stevens stared wide-eyed at the broken mask, then turned to the Hardys.

"Stick around, would you? I'd like somebody to help me explain what happened."

Frank peered out at the few remaining members of the crowd. "You've got several witnesses."

Stevens glanced back at the fallen mask. "That's good," he said. "Because I know one thing—the police aren't going to believe me."

An hour later the theater was almost empty—the police had released most of the audience members. Finally an officer approached Frank and Joe.

"I'm Lieutenant Kurt Ash," the burly officer said. "I'd like you to tell me exactly what happened."

He jotted down some notes as they spoke.

When Joe mentioned the metal hooks that had been sawed through, Lieutenant Ash stopped writing to stare at him with a doubtful expression.

"Interesting theory," he said skeptically. He closed his notebook and started to walk away.

Joe felt his temper flare. "Wait a minute!" he shouted, catching up with the officer. "That's it? People are almost killed, Ramsey's on the loose—"

"Hold it, kid," Ash interrupted. "You know why that mask fell? It was part of Stevens's little stunt for it to shake loose. And Ramsey—personally, I think Stevens arranged his appearance, too. Mark Stevens loves publicity. Every cop in town knows that."

Shoving his notebook in his rear pocket, Ash stomped off.

"I don't care what he says," Joe told Frank. "Ramsey was no publicity stunt."

"I don't know, Joe," Frank said. "Lieutenant Ash said Stevens has a reputation for pulling—" Frank stopped talking as Stevens joined them. He was carrying two books with him.

"I owe you two a lot," Stevens said. "The least I can give you is an autographed book." Opening the first book's cover, he asked, "What's your name?"

"Joe Hardy. This is my brother, Frank."

Stevens paused, his pen held over the title page. "Hardy? Any relation to Fenton Hardy, the detective?"

"We're his sons," Frank explained.

"I need to talk with your father," Stevens said. Glancing around to make sure no one was listening, he added, "Someone is trying to kill me. It's not just the mask. Other things have been happening, too."

"Dad's out of town, but we can help. We're detectives, too," Joe said. "If you're worried about Deke Ramsey—"

"It might be Ramsey," Stevens said, his face grim. "*If* it's human," he added mysteriously.

Before they could respond, Robert Lipp joined them from the backstage area. "Joyce has gone back to her office," the balding man said. "Are you ready to leave?"

15

Stevens closed the first book without having written anything. "Look, why don't you come out to my house for supper tonight?" he said to Frank and Joe. "I can explain then."

Remembering the angry police officer, Frank didn't answer. What if the incident onstage was really a part of another publicity stunt?

Joe didn't have the same reservations. "Great," he said. "We'd love to come."

Flipping to a blank page at the back of one of the books, Stevens drew them a map. "I'll see you at seven," he said. With Lipp at his side, he moved up the aisle and out of the theater.

Joe turned to Frank. "We've got a couple of hours to kill. What do you want to do?"

"We've got some clean clothes in the van," Frank said. "Let's change and then find the town library. I want to see what Mark Stevens has been up to."

The Ashfork Public Library was a cream-colored building located near the center of the business district. Inside, its shelves of books and off-white walls reminded Joe of every other library he'd ever seen.

Frank put another sheet of microfilm into the microfiche machine. Then he scanned the screen.

"It looks as if your favorite writer pulls a new stunt every time he has a book coming out,"

Frank said. "Once he had zombies invade a TV talk show."

Joe smiled.

"This one isn't so funny." Frank pointed to the machine's screen. "Last year someone reported him missing. The police thought he was kidnapped."

Joe whistled softly. "No wonder the cops are tired of him." Leaning forward, he read the article. "It says here that it turned out he was on vacation. Stevens claimed he didn't know anything about the stunt."

"Yeah, right," Frank said doubtfully.

"It won't hurt to listen to his story," Joe insisted. Checking his watch, he added, "We better get going. It's kind of a long drive to Stevens's house."

Frank returned their supplies while Joe left to get their van. Minutes later Frank went outside and climbed into the van.

With Joe behind the wheel, they took off and went past the city limits. Soon they found themselves surrounded by rolling hills and green pastures, with no other building or person in sight.

"How much longer?" Frank asked.

"We should be almost there," Joe said. His stomach growled, reminding him that he hadn't eaten for hours.

There was a turnoff up ahead. Joe slowed the van as they approached this new road. A sign had been posted beside it. It warned: Private Property! Do Not Enter!

"This must be the place," Joe said, and he steered the van down the long private drive. As they came out of a curve, the van's headlights fell across the stone facade of an enormous old house. Three stories high, the gothic-style mansion loomed in the gathering darkness. Strips of moss, which looked to Frank like many bony fingers, clung to the cut granite blocks. Two towers jutted up from the roof like horns.

"Makes quite an impression, doesn't it?" Joe asked.

"I'll say," Frank agreed.

Joe pulled the van to a stop. As they climbed out, Frank pointed to the roof lit with small spotlights.

Concrete gargoyles were mounted along the building's roofline. The gargoyles' lips were drawn back in evil sneers as they glared down on all visitors.

"Our welcoming committee," Frank said.

The mansion's front door swung open, and Mark Stevens stepped out onto the porch. "You're right on time," he said. "Welcome to Nightmare House."

"Nightmare House?" Frank shot a look at his brother.

Joe grinned and shrugged nonchalantly.

Stevens escorted them inside. The front hall was dark, just as Frank had expected. An ornate tapestry hung on the back wall, and a dramatic and sweeping staircase curved up to the second floor on the left. The handrail had a wolf's head carved into it.

Huge oil paintings lined the right wall, and all of them were particularly gruesome. Joe recognized one as being the cover of one of Stevens's books.

"It's—very nice," Frank commented.

"Just wait," Stevens promised.

He led them past the oils into the dining room. Compared to the center hall, Joe found it surprisingly simple—wooden floors and white walls. Too much gore must not be good for the appetite, Joe thought.

Two other guests were seated at the long dining table. Frank recognized the short, balding man—Robert Lipp, Stevens's agent. Joe's attention was focused on the girl at the opposite side of the table.

Lipp held out his hand. "Glad you could make it."

"The Lip has helped make me rich and famous," Stevens said.

"While I've become old and gray," Lipp retorted quickly. It was said as a joke, but it made Frank wonder. Lipp didn't look well. There were dark circles under his eyes, and his skin had a sickly pallor.

"I've been visiting for the last week," the

agent said. "But I'm also here to nag. It's time for Mark to finish his book."

"He's also my conscience," Stevens remarked.

"I'm Bev Hart," the girl seated at the table spoke up. "Mark's secretary." Joe couldn't help admiring her brown eyes and the way her short auburn hair framed her pretty face.

"Bev's only been with me for a year," Stevens declared, "but she's a gem. She types, proofreads, does research. She does everything on my books except write them. I keep promising to hire her some help. She needs an assistant."

Frank and Joe took their places at the table as a smiling woman wearing an apron entered the room. "Our guests have arrived, Michelle," Stevens told her. "Let's eat."

"Yes, sir," Michelle said, giving the Hardys a friendly glance. Michelle was middle-aged, her dark hair streaked with silver. Frank noticed the deep laugh lines around her blue eyes.

Michelle brought out the platters of food. Between mouthfuls of veal scaloppine, Stevens explained that his staff lived at the mansion. "Inspiration can strike at any moment—and so can the need for a cup of hot cocoa. Isn't that right, Michelle?"

Carrying a basket of hot dinner rolls, she responded with a wink.

As Joe finished his meal, he realized that Stevens hadn't said why he felt he was in danger. Michelle took his plate away and replaced it with dessert, chocolate mousse covered with raspberry sauce. Joe watched with regret as Bev excused herself and left the table before eating dessert.

Lipp remained in his seat. "Your young rescuers here aren't just fans," he told Stevens. "You're hiding something from me. What is it?"

"Bev and Michelle don't need to know this," Stevens said, lowering his voice, "but the Hardys are detectives."

Lipp frowned skeptically. "Do you really think you need detectives, Mark? Someone is only trying to scare you."

"I feel I need them, Robert," Stevens insisted.

"As you wish." Shaking his head, the agent stood up and walked out of the room.

Stevens faced the brothers. "I don't know where to begin," he said awkwardly.

"You said somebody was trying to kill you," Joe prompted.

"Somebody," Frank added, "or some *thing*."

"Pretty corny, huh?" Stevens's face grew red with embarrassment. "The strange thing is, it might be true. I know it sounds crazy."

"Go on," Joe prodded.

"The weird stuff began once I started my new novel," Stevens said with a sigh. "I decided to set the story in a secluded mansion. The mansion is dark stone. There are gargoyles on its roo—"

"It's like this house," Frank finished.

Stevens agreed. "In my story three people move into the house—an old man and his two nephews. Pretty soon they begin to think it's haunted. Strange things begin happening to them."

"Like what?" Joe asked.

Stevens took a deep breath. "Mirrors shatter spontaneously. The goldfish in their pond die. The garden withers. A heavy oil painting falls on the old man, almost killing him."

"You were almost struck by the falling mask," Joe pointed out. He could tell that the writer was badly shaken.

"Yes." Sweat beaded on Stevens's forehead. "That's not all. Three weeks ago I woke up to find that every mirror in the house had been broken. None of my staff heard a single sound during the night."

He pushed his chair back from the table. "Come outside with me."

Carrying a flashlight, Stevens led them through a rear door and out into the backyard. Stars were twinkling in the night sky.

Stevens turned the light on, shining it over a rose garden.

Joe touched one of the drooping dark red roses. Its petals fell under his touch. "It's dead."

Stevens nodded. "I wrote about flowers dying in my story, and now it's happened in my own garden. The gardener can't explain it." His voice dropped. "I don't know if I can finish my manuscript. Too much of it is coming true!" There was panic in his voice.

"Has there been anything else?" Frank asked.

"There's this," Stevens said in a voice so faint it was a whisper. Frank and Joe followed the flashlight's beam to another flower bed. The light played over a large tombstone that had been set among the dead flowers.

A gargoyle's head was perched on top of the tombstone. Words were carved into its granite surface:

STEVENS
REST IN PEACE

"Look at the date of death," Stevens said in a trembling voice. "It's two weeks from today!"

Chapter

3

IN THE MOONLIGHT Stevens's face was tight and drawn. As skeptical as Frank was of the writer's motives, he couldn't believe that Stevens was acting. The man was obviously scared to death.

"How long has the tombstone been here?" Frank asked.

"Five days," Stevens answered. "One morning after a thunderstorm, I looked out my window and there it was."

Taking the flashlight, Joe examined the ground around the tombstone. "Any footprints would have been washed away," he said.

"Are the grounds patrolled?" Frank asked.

"No," Stevens answered. "A fence runs around the property, but the gate doesn't lock. People come and go all the time."

"What about the mansion itself?" Joe asked. "Isn't it protected by a security system?"

"The best that money can buy," Stevens said. "But it didn't seem to help. My mirrors were shattered, anyway. It's as if there's an invisible enemy after me."

Frank studied him. "You don't really believe there are invisible evil spirits out to get you."

"No," Stevens admitted. "Even in my story, the incidents aren't being done by a ghost. There's a killer in the house. He's deranged and trying to scare the man and two boys."

"Does he succeed?" Joe asked curiously.

Stevens offered a wan smile. "Yes and no. In the end everybody dies."

The three of them started back to the mansion.

As he walked, Stevens said, "I don't know why, but someone is out to get me. Someone who knows every word as I write it, and then uses what he knows against me."

"You must have enemies," Frank said. "Deke Ramsey for one."

"As far as I know, Deke is my *only* enemy," Stevens said. "Besides, how would he know what's in my new book? Until today I hadn't seen him in ten years."

Stevens faced them. "I can't call the police in to help. They think this is just another publicity stunt. You said you could help. I'd like you to stay here at the mansion and investigate."

"Bayport isn't that far away," Frank said.

"I'd feel safer with you here."

Frank stepped up onto the back porch. "I don't know—"

"Why don't we spend the night and decide in the morning?" Joe said, cutting his brother off.

Under the porch light Frank could see that Joe was enthusiastic. He knew what Joe was thinking—with school still out, this was the perfect time to tackle a new mystery.

If this really is a mystery, Frank thought grimly. "All right," he said.

"Fantastic," Stevens said, acting relieved. "I'd hoped you'd stay. Michelle has prepared a room for you."

He took the Hardys up to the second floor and led them down a long hall where a collection of armor and medieval weapons was displayed. He left them at their bedroom door. The enormous room was almost dungeonlike despite its vastness. It had thick stone walls and a low beamed ceiling with a giant walk-in fireplace. Two beds took up most of one wall, and a massive wooden armoir occupied a second. The windows were little more than narrow slits in the thick stone walls.

"Check this out," Joe said, moving over to one of the windows. An enormous bunch of dried garlic hung above the window. "You think Stevens is expecting vampires? Isn't that why you hang garlic at your window—to keep vampires away."

Frank glanced at the other windows. Garlic had been hung above all of them. "I guess we should leave it up. Just in case," he joked.

Joe leaned forward to look out the window and noticed iron bars outside. Despite Stevens's apparent fear of vampires, it was impossible for a person to get in the window. Or out, either, Joe realized.

"You think the garlic's weird? Look at this," Frank said. Joe turned and saw his brother standing at the fireplace. Two skulls with candles inside were perched on top of the mantel, one on either end. Frank lifted one up to look at the bottom.

"It's ceramic," he said. He set it down and plopped down on one of the beds. "You know, Joe, this could all be a scam."

"If it is, we'll find out soon enough," Joe said. "But what if it isn't?"

Frank frowned. That was the problem. If it wasn't some kind of stunt, then Stevens's life could really be in danger.

"I guess we could stay a few days," Frank said. "At least until we check things out."

"That's great," Joe said happily.

"But I want to bring Callie in on this," Frank added.

"Callie?" Joe's smile faded. Frank's girlfriend, Callie Shaw, had helped on a few of their cases in the past. He didn't see any reason to bring her in this time, though.

"Stevens said he needs a new office assistant," Frank said. "Callie would fit in perfectly. When we're not around, she could keep an eye on Bev and Michelle. And Stevens."

Frank looked around and found the phone on the table between the beds. "I'll give her a call."

The next morning Stevens appeared at their bedroom door. "We decided to stay," Joe told him.

"I'd like to see about bringing someone in to help us," Frank said. He explained about having Callie pose as a new member of the staff.

"Fine," Stevens agreed quickly. "I'll hire her as a temporary assistant."

At the breakfast table Stevens told Lipp, Michelle, and Bev that he had hired Callie through an employment service the day before. "I've asked Frank to pick her up," he told the others.

"Will our guests be staying, then?" Michelle asked.

"The Hardys are good luck," Stevens declared. "They're welcome as long as they'd like to stay. And so is Callie. Michelle, please get a room ready for her."

Michelle seemed pleased by the announcement.

"We're writing a research paper for extra credit this summer," Frank said. "It's supposed to be on a famous living American author." This was the cover story he and his brother had decided to use. "Mr. Stevens said he'd be our subject."

"We'll want to talk to everyone who works for him," Joe said, watching for Bev's reaction.

"It's time I started working," she announced, getting up from the table.

After the others had gone, Frank and Joe walked out to the van. "After you get Callie, why don't you stop by the house," Joe told him, "and get some clothes."

"Sure you don't want to come?" Frank asked.

"Positive," Joe said. "I want to check this place out."

Frank raised an eyebrow. "This wouldn't have anything to do with a certain secretary?"

"What secretary?" Joe asked innocently.

"Just don't forget we're on a case." Frank started the van's engine. After putting the vehicle in gear, he drove down the driveway and away from the mansion.

Before going to Bayport, Frank took a detour over to Ashfork Granite and Marble. It was the only monument company in the area. If the tombstone in Stevens's yard had been ordered locally, it had to have come from there.

Frank found a parking space at the edge of the cluttered lot. In the middle of the work yard was a small office building, surrounded by marble cherubs and polished stone slabs. The office door opened as Frank stepped down from the van.

A tall man with stooped shoulders stood at the office door. The name tag on his shirt read Bill. "No solicitors," he said.

"I'm not a salesman." Speaking quickly, Frank described the purpose of his visit.

Scratching at the stubble on his chin, Bill nodded. "Yeah, I remember that one. Come on in."

The office was tiny, with green walls and a stained tile floor. A large metal desk occupied most of the space, with an upright filing cabinet taking up the rest.

Bill walked over to the filing cabinet and pulled out a piece of paper. "Here it is," he said. "The order was mailed in. Paid for with cash, too. The envelope was stuffed with it."

"Who placed the order?" Frank asked.

"Who?" Bill gave him a puzzled glance. "Mark Stevens. Who else?"

Frank took the sheet in his hand. The order had been typed on a piece of Stevens's personal stationery. In the place for the signature the writer's name had been typed.

"I figured it had to be a gag," Bill said.

"Who picked up the tombstone?" Frank asked.

Bill ran a dirty finger along a line on the page and read, " 'Pickup instructions—Leave outside gate.' "

"Must have been after hours," Bill said.

Frank held up the sheet of paper. "Can I keep this?"

Bill shrugged. "Sure. I don't need it anymore."

Frank took the paper and returned to the van. He backed it out of the yard and onto the street. Pulling around an old parked convertible, he guided the van back into traffic.

Frank felt more confused than ever. If Stevens was setting up an elaborate hoax, why would he use his own stationery to order the tombstone? It just didn't make sense.

The sheet of paper could be important. Frank doubted that he'd find a stray fingerprint on it, not after the way it had been handled, but it was his first real lead. When he got back to the mansion, he'd find out who had access to the paper. Stevens and Bev, certainly, and probably Michelle. But who else?

Frank tried to concentrate on the road ahead of him. The long stretch between Ashfork and Bayport was almost deserted.

His eyes flicked to the rearview mirror. There was only one other car running on the road behind him.

It was an old, battered convertible. Its dented body and torn cloth top seemed strangely familiar. Frank sat up sharply. He'd seen that car parked outside Ashfork Granite and Marble!

It could be a coincidence, he thought, but decided to find out for sure.

Signaling, he turned left on the next road. Dropping back, the convertible took the same turnoff.

In his mirror Frank could see that the convertible was missing its front license plate. A lone man rode in the front seat—a man Frank had never seen before.

Frank cranked the steering wheel hard, and the van slid over the blacktop before shooting onto a gravel lane.

The convertible almost missed the turn. It braked with a loud squeal. Its driver backed the car up, then turned it to follow the van.

"Definitely *not* a coincidence," Frank muttered.

Since he was being tailed, he couldn't risk going to Callie's. Besides, he wanted to see if the convertible had a rear license plate.

An idea came to him. Frank stomped on the gas pedal. The van jumped, rocketing ahead.

The convertible was rapidly outdistanced. The van roared away from the car, disappearing over the crest of the next hill.

Once he was out of sight, Frank eased the van off the road. He parked behind some tall shrubs, making certain he couldn't be seen.

Frank peeked out and watched as the convertible chugged up the hill.

The driver stopped at the top, and Frank

watched as a large man got out of the car and looked around. Seeing nothing, the husky stranger climbed back into the driver's seat, turned the car around, and drove back down the hill in a cloud of fumes.

Frank didn't bother to write down the car's license number. As junky as it was, the convertible had a personalized license plate.

The plate was stamped RAMSEY.

Ramsey—as in Deke Ramsey, Frank thought. What connection did he have with the beefy thug in the car?

"I've got plenty of questions," Frank muttered. "I wish I had some answers."

The hiss of escaping air broke Frank's concentration. Leaning out of the window, he saw a nail sticking out of the van's left rear tire. The tire was slowly going flat.

Frank groaned. This was the last thing he needed.

After hopping out of the van, he opened the back doors, pulled out the jack, placed it under the rear bumper, and cranked it up.

"Hey, punk," a strange voice rasped.

Frank looked up.

The thug had returned. He stood at the front of the van, a self-satisfied smirk on his face. His convertible wasn't in sight.

Seeing him up close, Frank realized that the man wasn't much older than he was. Black-haired and stocky, he had his eyes hidden behind mirrored sunglasses.

"You almost got away from me," the thug said, raising a baseball bat in one thick-fingered hand. "Looks like your luck just ran out."

After seeing Frank off, Joe went back inside the mansion.

Stevens was alone at the dining room table. "I'm not that eager to work on my novel," the writer confessed.

"When you write a book, do you follow an outline?" Joe asked.

"Yes," Stevens replied. "Why?"

"I'd like to see it," Joe said. "If someone's following it, I need to know what's going to happen next."

"Of course." Stevens set his cup of coffee down. "I'll have Bev make you a copy."

A few minutes later Joe went up to the secretary's office and knocked on the door.

"I thought it might be you," Bev said, opening the door. Remaining in the doorway, she handed him a manila envelope. "Mr. Stevens called on the intercom. He said to give you this."

Joe lifted the flap of the envelope. The story outline was inside.

"Usually I only send these to Mr. Stevens's publisher and publicist," Bev said. She viewed

Joe with suspicion. "You should be honored. You're the first fan to receive one."

She started to close the door. Joe caught it with his hand. "I'd like to ask you a few questions."

"Not now."

"It'll only take a minute," he promised.

"Didn't you hear me?" she snapped. "I'm busy!" She slammed the door in his face.

What was that all about? Joe wondered. He walked down the hall, trying to sort it out.

As he passed Stevens's office, he noticed that the door was slightly ajar. Gripping the doorknob, he gently pushed it in.

The mansion's housekeeper stood in the center of the room, her back to Joe. She was leaning over a massive mahogany desk.

"Michelle?" Joe asked.

"Oh!" The housekeeper jumped, whirling around. She relaxed when she saw Joe's face. "You frightened me."

"Is something the matter?"

"No, no. I—I was cleaning up, that's all." Michelle shoved her hand in her apron pocket. "I'm done now."

She stepped past Joe and hurried out. Joe wondered what was in her pocket.

Did living in the home of a horror writer make *everybody* weird? Joe wondered.

He glanced around the office. Plaques and awards seemed to be placed randomly on the walls. The room's only truly bizarre feature was the human skeleton mounted in one corner.

Joe went out and pulled the door closed behind him. He could hear Michelle's footsteps rushing down the stairs.

Joe followed the hallway to the stairs. I might as well find Michelle and talk to her now, he thought. It was as good a time as any.

A board creaked behind him. Joe started to turn when something heavy whooshed through the air right beside his ear. Then something hard slammed into his skull. His vision went black and his knees buckled. Joe pitched forward and tumbled endlessly down the stairs.

Chapter

4

FRANK WATCHED cautiously as the thug approached him. The man strutted forward, swinging the bat in a relaxed grip.

"You've made some kind of mistake," Frank said. He twisted sideways, keeping his right hand hidden behind his back. His fingers pressed around the jack.

"I don't think so," the thug said with a nasty smile.

As the man neared him, Frank jabbed at the jack's hydraulic pressure valve. Spewing air, it let the van drop. The rear wheel bounced to the ground, sending a cloud of dirt into the air.

"Hey!" the thug cried out. Startled, he jumped backward.

Frank took off running. He scrambled over an

embankment that led away from the road, sliding down its far side.

"Come back here!" the thug shouted.

At the bottom of the drop Frank checked for cover. There was heavy brush everywhere. He eased his way into a nearby thicket. Hidden among its leaves and branches, he hunched down and waited.

The thug hurried to the edge of the embankment. Clumsily he skidded down its far side. When he reached the bottom, he was covered with dirt.

Frank held his breath. By chance the thug had ended up directly in front of his hiding spot.

"I know you're here somewhere," the thug said, scanning the bushes.

Frank stayed in place, unmoving. The thug walked several feet back and forth.

Frank waited for him to turn his back. Finally he did. Swinging the bat onto his shoulder, the man started walking away.

Now! Frank thought.

Leaping out from the brush, he shoved the thug forward. The man stumbled and fell to his knees, dropping his weapon and losing his sunglasses. Frank kicked the bat a safe distance away. Catching the man's wrist, Frank brought his arm up behind his back.

"Owww!" the man protested.

"Who are you?" Frank demanded. "Why were you following me?"

"Figure it out yourself, hotshot," the thug sneered.

His eyes were a startlingly vivid gray. Deke Ramsey's eyes had been the same color, Frank remembered. Looking closer, he saw a strong resemblance between the two men. They shared the same muscular build, the same hard features.

"You're Ramsey's son!" Frank exclaimed.

"What of it?" The thug strained against Frank's grip. "You're hurting my arm, man."

"Why were you following me?" Frank asked.

Ramsey's son quit struggling. "Let me go and I'll tell you."

Frank considered it. He knew that he had to release the man sooner or later. At least he might get some information.

Frank let the man go. "Don't try anything."

Massaging his wrist, the thug dropped into a sitting position. He watched Frank warily.

Frank threw the baseball bat into the undergrowth. "What's your name? Why were you following me?"

"I'm Carl. Carl Ramsey. I followed you because you're working for Mark Stevens, and I'm not going to let you help him destroy my father."

Frank's jaw dropped. "What?"

"Stevens is a thief," Carl said. "He stole the idea for his first hit book from my father, and I'm not going to let it happen again."

"I don't know what you're talking about," Frank stated.

Carl viewed him uncertainly. "Well, maybe you don't," he said. "Let me fill you in."

Bitterly Carl told his story. Years earlier his father had been a successful horror novelist. Stevens was just starting out in those days. Everything between the two writers had been friendly at first.

"But then Stevens came out with *Colors of the Dead*," Carl continued. "A horror novel written for a teenage audience—the audience that my dad had built. Stevens's book was about an inner-city gang, recruiting new members. The twist was, the gang members had all been killed, years before . . . but they'd come back to life. Gruesome stuff."

"I've heard about that book," Frank said.

Carl nodded. "You probably did. It got a lot of publicity. It sold hundreds of thousands of copies."

"Your father had to expect competition," Frank said.

"You don't understand," Carl told him. "Dad didn't pay any attention to Stevens's success. He was busy finishing his own novel. It was the best thing he'd ever done, but nobody wanted it. You see, it was about an inner-city gang— back from the dead. My father had started that book a year before Stevens's book was published."

"It was a coincidence," Frank protested. "You can't blame another writer for that."

"Coincidence?" Carl scoffed. "The storylines were almost identical. Stevens stole the idea for *Colors of the Dead* from my father!"

"Do you have proof?"

"Not the kind you'd want," Carl answered. "But it happened, whether you believe it or not. Mark Stevens made a fortune, and my dad didn't get a thing. His readership fell, and his publisher dropped him. Now, just when he's working on a comeback novel, Stevens writes the same book. Stevens is a thief, and somehow he stole my father's idea once again. I'll do anything I can to help my father—whatever it takes!"

With that, Carl flung his arm up, hurling a handful of dirt into Frank's face. Blinded, Frank staggered away from him.

He brushed at his eyes, blinking until most of the grit was gone. It was too late, of course. Carl was escaping, scrambling over the top of the embankment as Frank watched from below.

Frank was left with more questions than ever. He wondered if Carl Ramsey was watching Nightmare House. That would explain how he'd followed Frank. Did that mean Ramsey was behind the attacks on the household?

Another question nagged at Frank as he climbed the embankment back to his van. Was Deke Ramsey a liar—or was Mark Stevens a thief?

* * *

"Mr. Hardy!" Someone was leaning over Joe. "Are you all right?"

Slowly everything swam into focus for him. Battered and dizzy, Joe lay sprawled at the bottom of the stairs. "Michelle?"

The housekeeper stood over him, shock expressed on her face. "What a terrible fall! That ax from the weapon collection must have fallen and hit you so you fell down the stairs." She pointed to the landing above where a medieval ax with a short wood handle stood with its heavy, curved blade imbedded into the floor. "You could have been killed!"

Joe sat up and lifted his hand to his head. There was a nasty lump under his hair near the crown. He winced as the blood pounded against his skull. It felt as if a bowling ball were rolling back and forth inside his head. In fact, as he revived more, he felt that his entire body was sore from his fall. Still, it could have been worse. The ax could have sliced his head open!

Michelle helped Joe to his feet. Ignoring his protests, she led him into the drawing room.

Joe sank onto a sofa and massaged his right knee, which had also been bruised in the fall. Still feeling dizzy, he shook his head to try to wake himself up.

Joe noticed a bell jar on the coffee table. Inside the jar was a shrunken head. Joe laughed when he saw it. "My brain feels like it's been pickled, too."

"I want you to rest," Michelle ordered, bending down to peer into his eyes, checking for a possible concussion. "Stay on that couch. I'll make you a cup of tea."

"I dropped an envelope," Joe told her, remembering the outline Bev had given him.

"I'll get it." As Michelle straightened up, a folded sheet of paper slipped from her apron pocket.

Joe remembered the woman's odd behavior in Stevens's office. Covering the paper with his foot, he slid it out of view.

When Frank returned to the mansion with Callie, he found Joe propped up on the sofa, reading the outline of Stevens's new book.

"A real man of action," Callie teased.

"That's not fair," Joe answered. "I'm in the middle of an investigation."

"What are you investigating?" Frank asked. "The sofa?"

Joe took the ribbing with a grin. "The stairs," he said.

Speaking softly, he told them about his fall. "Michelle says the ax fell. I'm wondering if it was dropped," he concluded grimly.

"Who was upstairs with you?" Frank asked.

"Bev and Michelle," Joe said. "Lipp, too, I guess. Michelle says he's resting in his room. I

43

don't know where Stevens was. He wasn't in his office.''

"There's something else to consider," Frank said. "Someone might have bypassed the mansion's security system. Someone like Deke Ramsey."

He told them about his encounter with Carl Ramsey. "I doubt that Stevens has to steal ideas, but I'd like to know for sure," Frank concluded.

"We can't just come out and ask," Joe pointed out.

"Let me see what I can find out," Callie said. "Once I start working, I'll check Stevens's files. Every writer keeps notes."

Frank brought out the tombstone order that he'd taken from the monument company. "This was written on a piece of Stevens's stationery. Do you see anything unusual about it?"

Joe took the sheet of paper. "It was done on a manual typewriter."

"How can you tell?" Callie asked.

"Some of the letters are darker than the others." Joe gave her the sheet. "That doesn't happen on an electric machine or a computer printer."

"Why?" Callie asked.

"The old manuals wore unevenly—the wear depended on who used it," Frank explained. "The typeface can be as distinctive as fingerprints. On this machine the lowercase *s* has been banged up. It doesn't print clearly. Find a typewriter key with similar wear, and you'll know what machine it was printed on."

"The tombstone might be the least of our worries," Joe said. He waved the outline for Stevens's new novel. "I've been reading through this, and there's a whole list of things that might happen if the culprit is really using it as an outline for his or her attacks."

"Like what?" Frank demanded.

Joe looked at him grimly. "Beheadings. Poison. A desk drawer full of deadly, poisonous vipers waiting to bite the first hand that reaches inside—"

Callie shuddered.

"And in the end the entire house catches fire and burns to the ground," Joe concluded.

Before he could discuss the outline further, he heard footsteps enter the room behind him. "Ah," Mark Stevens said. "My new assistant!"

"Mr. Stevens," Callie replied politely. Still holding the sheet of stationery in her hand, she asked, "Do you own a manual typewriter?"

"Not me," he answered. "I use a word processor. Why do you ask?"

"Just curious." Callie tucked the paper into her purse. Frank knew she'd check it against the machines in the house—just in case.

Stevens beamed at them. "I've spent my morning working in the basement," he said.

"It's my favorite room of the house. Would you like to see it?"

"The basement?" Callie asked doubtfully.

"Sure," Joe said.

Stevens led them to the back of the mansion. Opening a door, he guided them down a flight of concrete steps.

The basement was pitch-black.

Stevens's voice floated to them from out of the darkness. *"This* is why my home is called Nightmare House," he said dramatically.

Fluorescent lights flickered on. Callie gasped and moved closer to Frank.

Joe's eyes lit up. What was in front of him was like a scene from a horror movie. Cobwebs drifted down from the ceiling, and leaning against the back wall was a coffin. A guillotine stood just in front of them, its shiny blade raised, poised ready to drop. Behind that was an iron maiden, black and casketlike, and a wooden rack. Two sets of manacles were on the rack, ready to imprison a helpless victim.

"It's a torture chamber," Frank said.

"Impressive, isn't it?" Stevens glowed with pride. "Exact reproductions, I assure you. And every piece a work of art." He lovingly ran a hand over his scale-model guillotine.

Joe walked over to the machine. Its blade was supported by two tall upright guides. It had a bench to lie on and a place to rest a prisoner's neck for beheading.

"Be my guest," Stevens said to Joe, gesturing toward the bench.

Joe touched the guillotine's sharp blade. "Does it work?"

"Oh, no," Stevens assured him. He lifted his hand to a lever at the side of the guillotine. "This releases the blade," he said. "But it doesn't work. Even if I were to pull it, nothing would happen." He grinned mischievously. "Lie down on the bench and I'll show you."

"Don't do it," Callie said nervously.

Joe winked at her as he lay down on the bench. He stretched out on his back, resting his head and neck beneath the heavy blade.

"That's enough—" Frank started to say.

Stevens started to cackle hideously. Looking up, Joe saw him jiggle and pull at the release lever.

Suddenly he wiggled the lever free.

Frank watched in horror as the deadly guillotine blade fell straight for Joe's exposed neck.

Chapter
5

"JOE!" Callie screamed.

The guillotine blade sliced downward. Joe didn't have time to escape—the sharp edge was almost at his throat.

Without warning the blade slammed to a stop, blocked by a hidden catch in the woodwork.

Stevens stopped cackling and began to roar with laughter. "You should see your faces!"

Frank spun around and turned on the writer. "That was a joke?"

"It wasn't very funny," Callie said tensely.

Joe squeezed out from under the blade and sat up on the bench, shaking slightly. "No, it sure wasn't."

Stevens's laughter died away as he took in the three angry faces. "I'm sorry," he said contritely. "I didn't mean any harm. It was only a prank."

"He plays it on all of his visitors," said a voice from the basement stairs.

Turning, they saw Robert Lipp standing on the steps. "You're wanted upstairs, Mark," the agent said. "Joyce Halloran is here to see you."

"My publicist?" Stevens asked, frowning.

"You had an appointment," Lipp reminded him. "She's brought a reporter from the *Gazette*."

Stevens moaned. "I forgot all about it." Reluctantly he followed Lipp up the steps.

As soon as the two men were gone, Frank spoke out. "How could Stevens pull a joke like that when he's supposedly scared for his life?"

"That's just the way he is," Joe said in a calming voice. "He's a big kid. One look around this house and you know that."

"Maybe," Frank said skeptically.

Joe pulled a creased sheet of paper from his pants pocket. "I almost forgot to look at this," he told the others. "It fell out of Michelle's pocket."

He spread the paper open. Large individual printed letters had been glued onto the sheet.

Frank and Callie leaned over it for a better look. "I will cut out your heart," the paper read.

Callie's eyes widened. "Wow."

"Look at the letters," Frank said. They were

all different sizes and printed on glossy paper. "The letters were cut out of magazines."

"I wonder why Michelle had it?" Callie said.

"I walked into Stevens's office while she was cleaning," Joe said. "When she saw me, she slipped something into her apron. I guess it was the note."

"Maybe she found it in there," Callie suggested.

"Or maybe she was about to leave it there," Frank said. Joe nodded. Refolding the death threat, he returned it to his pocket.

"Miss Shaw?" a frosty voice inquired. Bev stood above them on the basement steps.

Callie stared at her, confused. "That's Stevens's secretary," Frank whispered.

Bev refused to look at the Hardys. "If you're done visiting," she told Callie, "it's time to go to work."

Turning on her heel, Bev marched up the last stairs. With an apologetic gesture to the others, Callie hurried after her.

"If I didn't know better, I'd think Bev was avoiding me," Joe said.

Frank clapped his brother on the back. "True love isn't easy."

"True love?" Joe said. "I'd settle for true like."

Frank wandered through the basement, examining the various displays. "Replicas or not, some of these are pretty dangerous."

"It's all part of the image," Joe said.

Frank stopped before the iron maiden. The tall metal box was formed in the shape of a woman. Its single door held long iron spikes that protruded inward. Frank knew that in ancient times a captive would be put inside the box. When the door was closed, the spikes would impale the victim. No wonder it looks like a coffin, he thought.

"We'd better get back to work," Joe said, breaking Frank's train of thought.

"Yeah," Frank agreed. "Let's start by walking around the property."

"After that I want to show you the outline of Stevens's novel," Joe said. "Parts of it are pretty intense." After reading the outline Joe was more concerned than ever because in the wrong hands it could be a recipe for murder.

Frank switched off the lights, and the boys went up the basement steps.

"Let me get my jacket," Frank said in the front hall. Grabbing the banister, he started up the stairs to the second floor. After a few steps he stopped and indicated he was listening.

"What is it?" Joe whispered.

Frank motioned for him to come closer. Joe crept up beside him.

The boys could hear raised voices from the second floor. A man was shouting, his exact words muffled by the distance.

Together, the Hardys ran up the stairs. Reaching the top landing first, Frank saw the publicist and her reporter hastily retreating from Stevens's office. They'd just backed out of the room when the door was banged shut in front of them.

Standing in the hallway, the publicist clutched the reporter's pudgy arm. "I'm sorry, Tim. Mr. Stevens isn't usually like this."

Sloppily dressed and big-bellied, Tim shrugged. "No problem, Joyce," he said. "At least I've got a story."

"What story?" Joyce asked, alarmed.

Tim pulled his arm away. He lifted his hands as if he were framing a headline. " 'The Haunting of Nightmare House.' "

"You can't print that!" Joyce noticed the Hardys and threw them a pleading glance. "I'll be fired!"

"Sorry." After heading for the stairway, the reporter found it blocked by Frank. Joe stood right behind him.

"Move it, kid," Tim said.

Frank didn't budge. Looking at the publicist, he asked, "What's up?"

"I've made a mess of things," Joyce blurted out. "Mr. Stevens has decided he doesn't want any more publicity, but I'd—I'd—"

"You'd already talked to this reporter," Joe said.

"It's my job!" she wailed. "I'm a publicist. I'm *supposed* to talk with the press!"

"Joyce told me what's been happening," Tim said smugly. "The broken mirrors, the ghostly tombstone—everything. Publicity stunt or not, it'll make a great feature story."

He pushed past the Hardys. Joyce watched him go, a crushed expression on her face.

She hadn't meant any real harm, Joe knew. He went after the reporter, catching up to him.

"What if I gave you a real scoop?" he told him in a hushed voice. "What if I told you who was behind the haunting—and why?"

"Yeah?" Tim said. "How would you know?"

"Have you ever heard of Fenton Hardy?" Joe asked in the same hushed tone.

Tim's brow wrinkled in thought. "The big-shot detective?"

"That's right." Putting an arm around the reporter, Joe guided him farther down the stairs and away from Joyce. "We're his sons. My brother and I are working on a case for him. Give us a few days and you'll have a story you can put on the front page."

"A front-page piece?" Tim's eyes narrowed greedily. "If you're Hardy's son, prove it. Let me see your driver's license." Joe pulled out his wallet and passed over his license.

"Joe Hardy, huh?" Tim nodded to himself. "Okay, you've got a deal. I'll give you five days to come up with something. After that I'm submitting my original story."

With that, Tim plodded down the last few steps and out the front door.

Joe walked back up to Frank and Joyce.

"He's decided not to run the story for a few days. He wants to see what else develops."

Joyce gave a relieved sigh. "Thanks for the reprieve," she said. "Your brother just told me you're both staying here for a bit. Thanks again for coming to my rescue. I hope that Mr. Stevens calms down soon." After sweeping down the stairs, she left the house.

Joe gave Frank a summary of his conversation with the reporter. "Five days?" Frank said incredulously.

"It's not going to be easy," Joe admitted.

They walked down the hall to Stevens's office. Inside, Frank could hear the sound of another growing argument. Turning the doorknob, he pushed the door open.

Mark Stevens was inside, red-faced with anger. Robert Lipp was staring back at him, obviously just as upset. They barely seemed to notice the Hardys entering the room.

"I don't need this aggravation," Stevens snapped to his agent.

"You've always liked publicity before," Lipp replied. "It's a mistake to cut it off now. Give the reporter a story."

"A story?" Stevens's eyebrows shot up. "The story is, someone is out to kill me! Imagine what will happen if *that* gets in the papers. I'll never finish this book if reporters start following me around!" Stevens just shook his head. To Frank, it seemed to be a sad gesture of defeat.

"Are you still scared that someone is out to get you?" Lipp asked the writer. "That's ridiculous. The things that have happened here are little more than pranks."

"I don't believe that," Stevens said. "The things I'm writing about are actually happening. I'm frightened."

Lipp rubbed his temples wearily. "And you think there's worse to come, is that it? Deadly falls, poisonings—murder?"

"Yes," Stevens said.

"I've seen the novel outline," Joe spoke up. "If someone is following it, the attempts will be more than pranks."

Lipp took a pitcher off Stevens's desk and poured himself a glass of water. "What do you think, Frank?" he asked.

"I don't know yet," Frank said.

"Foolishness, that's all this is." Lipp raised the glass and took a sip.

The water dribbled down his chin as Lipp began choking. Dropping the glass, the man clutched at his chest and reached out with his other hand. He bumped the pitcher of water, and it smashed on the floor.

"I've been poisoned," Lipp croaked.

Frank stepped toward him and saw Lipp's eyes roll back in his head. Then the agent's legs gave way as he collapsed to the floor.

Chapter

6

FRANK QUICKLY KNELT over the fallen man. The agent's lips were white, and his face was beaded with sweat.

Stevens remained frozen in place.

Frank loosened Lipp's tie and collar. Joe felt for the agent's pulse.

"He's still alive," Joe said.

Joe's reassuring words stirred Stevens to action. The horror writer reached for the telephone and quickly dialed 911, demanding an ambulance.

Joe slipped a pillow under the agent's head. His coloring was slowly returning, and his breathing was shallow but regular.

The siren of an approaching ambulance sounded faintly in the distance. It grew louder as it approached. At last Frank saw Lipp's eyelids flutter and blink open.

"Wh-what happened?" he murmured.

"Thank goodness you're all right!" Stevens cried, dashing over to Lipp.

Lipp glanced around. "The water had a bitter taste," he said slowly. "I started to spit it out, but then don't remember what happened."

"This is all my fault," Stevens said angrily. "This situation is out of hand."

"I'm not quitting and leaving you," Lipp said forcefully. "You're my last client, Mark," he added quietly. "I've been with you from the start. I won't abandon you now."

"You win," he said with a sigh. "But remember your promise, Robert. After this book you'll retire."

"One more book," Lipp agreed, nodding weakly. "Let's make it the best one yet."

A few minutes later Michelle showed the medics into the study.

"I want you fully examined by a doctor," Stevens insisted as the attendants hoisted the stretcher with Lipp and carried him out to the ambulance.

Joe returned to the desk, where the shattered glass and pitcher lay. He carefully stepped around the shards of broken glass. He lifted one piece and sniffed at it. "I can't smell any kind of chemical or poison," he noted. "Maybe he just passed out. It seemed odd that he got better on his own."

"He might have just been scared and fainted, or his system could have been strong enough to fight the poison on its own."

"I'm mad because there's not enough here to send to a lab for testing," Frank remarked, checking out the wet spot on the carpet where the water had soaked in.

"It had to be poison," Stevens said glumly. "It's exactly the situation I wrote into my new novel—one of my characters becomes violently ill after drinking a glass of water. That water was poisoned, and it was intended for me. I'm only sorry Lipp was the victim instead of me."

At supper that evening Stevens explained that Lipp was going to be fine—the final results on the poisoning weren't in yet, though. Callie excused herself before coffee. "There's a ton of paperwork on my desk," she explained.

Bev dabbed at her mouth with a napkin. "I'll go with you."

Joe's eyes followed the secretary's retreating back. "Think they'd like some company? I don't drink coffee."

Frank grinned and decided against coffee, too. "I'll see what Michelle's up to," he whispered to his brother.

Joe went up to Bev's office. When he opened the door, he saw two desks, a personal computer, and several rows of filing cabinets. To his disappointment, he didn't see any of Stevens's horror-oriented oddities.

Sitting at her desk, Callie was reading through stacks of letters piled in front of her. "Hi, Joe," she said.

Bev lifted her head from her computer. "What do you want?" she asked.

"It's nice to see you, too," Joe replied in a low whisper.

Callie opened the flap of a large manila envelope and pulled out its contents. "This is a contract of some sort."

"What are you doing with that?" Rushing across the room, Bev snatched the envelope from Callie. "Your job is to answer the fan mail. That's all."

Joe felt his temper flare. "You don't have to be rude about it."

"We have work to do, Mr. Hardy," Bev said, dropping the contract back into its envelope. "Visiting hours are over."

Joe knew there had to be a reason why Bev was so unfriendly, but he couldn't think of it.

Shrugging his shoulders, Joe walked out of the office and bumped right into Frank.

"Whoa, slow down," Frank said. "Did you find out what's bugging Bev?"

"Nope. I don't have a clue. What did you find out?"

"It's Michelle's night off," Frank said, "and

she's leaving the mansion. Want to come follow her with me?''

Joe threw a last look at Bev's office. "You bet.''

Michelle drove away from Nightmare House in a late-model sedan. Piloting the van, Joe stayed well behind her. He was dismayed by the lack of traffic on the country road—he didn't have any cover. "This isn't going to be easy," he said.

"Just don't lose her," Frank told him.

Joe kept the red taillights of the sedan just in sight. A light fog had drifted in, which did provide a little cover for the van. Still, if the housekeeper was alert, Joe knew that she'd spot them.

After a few miles the sedan turned toward Ashfork's busy downtown area. Michelle slowed her car down and parked it in front of the Ashfork Cinema.

"There's no mystery in this," Joe commented. "She's going to see a movie."

"We might as well go back," Frank said.

As he watched, Michelle locked the car door. Pausing under the theater marquee, she glanced at her wristwatch. Her lips parted in mild alarm as she walked away from the ticket booth.

"Park it," Frank said urgently.

Joe twisted the steering wheel, guiding the van into a space. Frank threw open his door and leapt out.

Michelle was well ahead of him when she left the sidewalk and stepped into an alleyway.

Frank and Joe raced to catch up with her. Running into the dark alley, they found themselves surrounded by the outside walls of stores.

The alley was empty. "She's gone," Frank said. "Do you think she saw us?"

"Even if she spotted us," Joe said, "where could she go? This is a dead end."

Joe walked along one side of the alley, Frank the other. As Joe neared the back wall, he saw something. "Over here," he called to Frank. "There's a door here that's slightly ajar."

The metal door pushed in at his touch. Frank caught up with Joe, and the boys walked inside.

Joe heard the faint strains of music coming from the front of the building. There was also light up at the end of the long narrow hallway, which was blocked off by a thin curtain.

Suddenly the curtain was yanked aside. A hulking figure rushed toward them, a flashlight raised to shine in their direction. "What are you doing here?" the hulk growled.

Frank lifted his hand against the flashlight's glare. "We're looking for a friend."

"I'll bet," he said sarcastically. "Well, look for your friend out front. Customers aren't allowed to enter through the back."

"Customers?" Joe asked.

The man lowered his flashlight as he came closer. "We don't allow freebies," he said.

"You want to see the show, you'll have to pay the cover charge." Planting a meaty hand on each of their backs, he steered the Hardys back into the alley.

The door slammed shut behind them.

"He's big, he has an attitude, and he carries a flashlight," Frank said. "I think he's what you call a bouncer."

Joe reached for his wallet. "Come on. Let's go pay the cover charge."

After leaving the alley and circling around to the front of the building, the Hardys found themselves outside a blues club. As they entered the club, Frank watched as an entertainer took the stage.

"Joe!" Frank stared straight ahead, astonished.

Michelle was onstage, dressed in a sequined gown and holding a microphone. As the band began, she started to sing.

Joe stopped a passing waiter. "Who's performing tonight?"

"That's Michelle Taft," he replied. "She's here every Tuesday. Good, isn't she?" Shouldering a tray, the waiter left.

"Michelle looks different without a feather duster in her hand," Joe admitted.

"She's not your ordinary housekeeper," Frank agreed. "I wonder if she has any other secrets."

The Hardys were impressed with Michelle's

voice and singing ability. After her set, they went backstage. The dressing room had a star mounted on its closed door. Frank knocked at the door.

Michelle answered the knock. "Come in . . . Frank and Joe."

They entered the room. The housekeeper was sitting at a vanity, wiping makeup and cold cream from her face.

"How'd you know it was us?" Frank asked.

She spoke into the mirror, watching his reflection. "I saw your faces in the audience. You gave me quite a fright."

"Why?" Joe inquired.

"I knew you'd come to talk with me. You're detectives. Don't bother to deny it: I overheard Mr. Stevens talking about it. I know why you're here, too." She turned to face them. "You're here because of that ugly, awful letter."

"Joe found the sheet of paper after it fell from your apron pocket," Frank said.

"I'd never do anything to hurt Mr. Stevens," she told them. "That's the truth."

"But you had the death threat," Frank said.

Michelle took a deep breath. "It was all so stupid," she said. "I was cleaning the office, and I found that . . . *thing* on Mr. Stevens's desk. I didn't know what it was. When I picked it up and read it, I was horrified."

"You had it in your hand when I came into the office, didn't you?" Joe asked.

Michelle nodded. "I was afraid you'd think I was responsible for it, so I shoved it into my pocket. Then I lost it. . . ."

She raised her head, her brow furrowed. "It was a dreadful, dreadful mistake."

Frank wanted to believe Michelle, but he couldn't be sure she was telling the truth. "Why haven't you told anyone that you're a singer?" he asked.

"Not everyone approves of a singing maid," Michelle said slowly.

Frank was surprised. "Do you think Mark Stevens would fire you?"

"I don't know," she said uneasily.

It was almost midnight when the Hardys and Michelle returned to the mansion. Frank checked the grounds, and Joe made certain that the first-floor doors and windows were secure while Michelle went up to bed.

"No new headstones," Frank reported to Joe.

"Everything's locked up. I'll turn the security system on," Joe said, stifling a yawn.

Silently the brothers slipped upstairs to their bedroom, where Frank finally read Stevens's outline.

Sitting on his bed a few minutes later, Frank pulled his shoes off. "The way I figure, only one person benefits if Stevens can't finish his book. That's Deke Ramsey. If Ramsey really is writing a book about a haunted house, then he's got to get his published before Stevens does. Let's see if we can find him tomorrow.''

He was answered by the sound of deep, rhythmic breathing. Joe was asleep, fully clothed, on top of the covers.

Frank finished changing his clothes and climbed into bed. Very soon he felt himself drifting off to sleep.

Abruptly a loud scream pierced the air.

Frank was instantly awake and sitting up in his bed, the covers tossed aside.

''What was that?'' Joe asked groggily. ''Did somebody scream?''

''Not just somebody,'' Frank told him. ''That was Callie!''

Chapter
7

FRANK AND JOE raced out of their room and within seconds were at Callie's door. No other member of the household appeared, which surprised the boys.

Joe tried the doorknob. "It's locked!"

Frank hammered his fist against the door. "Callie! Open up!"

He heard the turning of the lock. Dressed in a long robe, Callie opened the door and peered out. "I'm glad it's you," she said with relief.

Shakily, she stepped forward. Frank put his arm around her. "Are you okay?" he asked, concerned. "You look as if you've seen a ghost."

"I don't believe it, but I think maybe I did," Callie said.

With a shiver she glanced at the room behind her. "Let's not talk in there."

"What happened?" Frank asked in the hallway.

"I was reading one of Mark's books and I guess I fell asleep. A few minutes ago I woke up and had the strangest feeling that someone was in the room with me."

"It was probably just a dream," Joe said. "After all, you'd been reading a horror novel."

"I was awake," Callie insisted. "I know I wasn't dreaming. And that's not all. While I was lying there, I heard a voice. The voice told me to leave Nightmare House—leave it or die!" She shuddered. "When I turned on the lights—no one was there!"

"What kind of voice?" Frank asked. "A man's or a woman's?"

Callie answered slowly. "It was low and muffled. Guessing, I'd say a man was talking."

"A man who vanished when the lights came on?" Joe asked doubtfully.

"I know it sounds ridiculous," Callie said.

Frank considered the situation. Callie wasn't the type to imagine things. "The voice could have come from a tape recorder—or even from someone hiding under the bed. We need to find out."

Frank took Callie's hand as they ducked back into her room.

After they'd searched everything else, Joe and Frank checked out the closet. "Nothing,"

Joe said. "Whoever was in here is long gone now."

"Wait, Joe." Frank was examining the back wall of the closet. "The bedroom walls are plastered, but the inside of the closet has been finished with expensive paneling. That doesn't make sense."

Joe studied the wood more closely. "I feel a breeze," he said all at once.

Frank was tapping against the back wall. "It sounds hollow behind this."

"There's definitely a draft rising up from the floor." Joe ran his hand along the bottom edge of the paneling.

Dropping to his knees, too, Frank found a small space between the baseboard and the paneling. He pushed his forefinger into the gap. "There's something in here," he told the others.

"What is it?" Callie asked.

"It's metal. It feels like a latch of some sort." Frank tugged at it with his finger. The latch pulled free. Frank snatched his hand away as the rear wall of the closet rolled open. "What in the world—?"

In the opening behind the closet was a brick-lined corridor. It led straight back for a few feet before turning out of sight. A low light flickered from around the bend.

"I can't believe it," Callie said. "A secret passageway? I thought they only had those in the movies!''

"Well, somebody probably used this passageway to creep into your closet and give you a scare," Joe told her.

Frank stood up. "Whoever it was left in a hurry. If the person had closed the passage properly, we wouldn't have found the opening."

"Well, we've found it now," Joe said. "Are you guys coming or not?"

Joe stepped into the narrow corridor, a cold chill settling over him. Walking single file, Frank and Callie followed him. "It's creepy in here," Callie said.

"You got that right," Frank whispered. He felt something brush against his forehead and looked up at the low ceiling. In the dim light he made out a long, dangling cobweb.

"Ouch!" Callie jumped back and peered at the wall beside her. "There's a sharp nail sticking out here. I almost cut myself!"

"Look at this!" Joe said excitedly. He was kneeling beside some dark splotches on the stone floor. He touched one of the splotches, examined his finger, and looked up at Frank and Callie. "Blood," he said.

"Let's keep going," Frank suggested.

Six feet farther along the hidden passage, Joe spotted more drops of blood on the floor and pointed them out.

As Joe rounded the corner, the corridor brightened. There were torches mounted on the wall up ahead. The heads of the torches were lit, the flames dancing eerily.

"I wonder why there isn't any soot on the ceiling?" Joe mused aloud. He sniffed the air. "I don't smell smoke, either."

"You're right." Frank studied the closest torch. Reaching up, he peeled back the covering that protected its base. A metal tube ran through its center. There was a knob mounted on its side.

Frank turned the knob. As he did, the flames dimmed. "It's a gas jet."

"Another of Mark Stevens's surprises," Joe said.

"I feel as if I've seen this before," Callie said. "The torches, the secret passage—it seems familiar."

"It reminds me of an old horror movie," Frank said.

Callie's eyes lit up. "Not an old movie," she said. "A recent one. *Banquet of Blood*. We saw it last summer."

Joe snapped his fingers. "You're right. And that film was adapted from a Mark Stevens novel."

"We know that Stevens is using Nightmare House as the setting for his new manuscript," Frank said. "I'll bet he used it for *Banquet,* too."

Joe followed the trail of blood. It led them

along the passageway as it circled through the upper two floors. Joe only found entrances off the passageway into the offices used by Bev and Stevens.

The last leg of the corridor brought them down to the bottom of the house. There, Joe lifted the latch that held the last panel in place. He, Frank, and Callie stepped out into the basement.

Frank found the light switch and flipped it on. There were a few more drops of blood on the basement floor—then no more. "From here our boogeyman could have gone anywhere," he said. "He could have been out the back door in minutes."

"But how did he get in?" Callie asked. "Wouldn't the alarm have gone off?"

Frank and Joe exchanged glances. Callie had a point. Either the alarm system had been by-passed—or her night visitor had been in the house all the time.

"Let's get some rest," Frank said. "Maybe it will all be clearer in the morning." They made their way back through the house to the second floor.

Frank and Joe returned with Callie to her bedroom. Together they moved the room's heavy maple dresser into the closet, blocking the passage entrance.

Joe stood back, dusting his hands. "I hope we don't have to move that thing again."

"At least we know that nobody else will be getting in here," Frank said.

"Thanks for the help," Callie told them. "Hey—I almost forgot."

Opening a dresser drawer, she removed a sheet of stationery and gave it to Frank. "I've checked the tombstone order against every typewriter in the house. None of them matches."

"Who uses the stationery?" Joe asked.

"Everybody. There's a supply of it in the library and in the office—it isn't hard to find." Callie blinked sleepily. "Good night, guys."

At breakfast the Hardys told Stevens that they'd stumbled across the secret passageway.

The writer was delighted. "How did you get into it?" he asked.

"We were in Callie's room," Joe said. "She was putting some clothes in the closet." With everyone at the table, he didn't want to say anything more.

Stevens nodded. "The catch is set too low. Bump against the wood that covers it, and it releases the inside latch."

Thinking back, Frank remembered the pattern of the paneling. One of the squares had been somewhat lighter in color. He guessed that pushing against it would have caused the wall to open as well.

"Does every secret panel have the same type of release?" Joe asked.

"Each one is different. It's more fun that way." Joe noticed that the writer appeared to be pleased with himself.

"How many people know about the secret passageway?" Callie asked.

Just then Bev entered the dining room. "Not too many. Just a few million fans, that's all." She threw them a cold smile. "I overheard your conversation as I was coming in."

"Joyce invited a camera crew out to film it," Stevens grumbled. "I never should have given my approval."

Just then Michelle came into the dining room, carrying a pitcher of orange juice.

"I hope I didn't disturb anyone last night," Callie said. "When the wall opened on me, I—well, to be honest, I screamed."

Frank raised his eyes, waiting for a reaction from the others. Callie had delivered her line perfectly, just as they'd planned. Now they'd find out why no one else had reacted to her cry.

"Bev and I have the rooms on the top floor," Stevens told her. "It's rare for either of us to hear anything from below. How about you, Michelle?"

"I'd been out late and must have just fallen asleep," Michelle answered.

Bev looked across the table at her employer.

"I have some bad news. I can't find the computer disks."

Stevens's eyes widened. "The ones that store my new novel?"

"Yes," Bev said. "But I know what's happened to them."

Stevens waited expectantly as Frank and Joe turned to her, too.

"Callie Shaw stole them!" Bev exclaimed.

Chapter

8

"CALLIE'S NOT a thief!" Frank said indignantly.

"I've been watching her," Bev insisted. "She doesn't act like a secretary. Instead of typing, she spends her time snooping through the desk drawers and filing cabinets."

Callie was speechless and sat in silence, nervously wringing the napkin in her hands.

"Last night I called the employment service we use. They've never even heard of Callie Shaw!"

"I—I didn't . . . I mean, I haven't—" Callie stammered hopelessly for a moment. She turned to Frank for help.

"When Mr. Stevens told us he needed a new assistant, we recommended Callie," Frank explained.

"Is that true, sir?" Bev asked Stevens.

Stevens slowly nodded his head. "Yes," he said. "Miss Shaw has been searching the files at my request. She was trying to find some documentation I needed." He patted his suit pocket. "She brought it to me right before breakfast."

"What about the computer disks?" Bev asked.

"I'm sure they'll turn up," Stevens replied confidently. But the troubled expression on his face told the Hardys that Stevens wasn't as certain as he pretended to be.

Stevens got up from the table. "Frank and Joe, please join me in the library."

Stevens entered the library, leaving its door open. Frank stopped Joe at the entrance, pulling him over to one side.

"Did you notice anything unusual about Bev this morning?" Frank asked.

"Other than her usual charm?" he asked.

Frank shook his head. "I almost didn't notice it because of the sleeve of her blouse, but she was wearing a bandage around her left arm just above the elbow."

Joe was puzzled. Then it dawned on him. "You mean she might have cut herself and left a trail of blood—"

"In the secret passageway." Frank nodded. "And I had another thought. Remember when

Bev said she'd been spying on Callie, watching her go through the desk drawers?"

"Sure," Joe said. "So?"

"Callie isn't careless," Frank said. "She wouldn't search a room unless she was all alone."

"Bev could have been watching from behind the hidden panel!" Joe said. "If she nudged it open just a crack, Callie wouldn't have noticed her."

"Right. It opens into the offices. Also, Bev's made it clear that she doesn't like Callie's being here," Frank said. "She probably sneaked into Callie's room last night."

"But why would Bev do something like that?" Joe asked.

"She might be afraid that Callie will steal her job," Frank replied. "Or maybe Bev has something to hide."

"Hardys?" came a voice. Stevens stood in the doorway, his hands on his hips. "Won't you *please* come in and talk with me?"

Frank and Joe walked into the library and took seats on the black leather couch. Bookcases lined the dark wood walls. The bookends, Joe noticed, were shaped like coffins.

"What have you found so far?" Stevens asked, pacing in front of the Hardys.

"Not enough." Frank gave Stevens a shortened version of their adventures.

Stevens was shaken by the account. "You're

wasting your time with Michelle and Bev. I trust them completely." His shoulders slumped. "You're no closer than before. What's worse, now my computer disks have disappeared!"

"Don't you have backup disks?" Frank asked. Frank made sure that whenever he used his computer, he copied the information onto a separate disk.

"The backups!" Stevens said. "I'd completely forgotten about them."

Considering the events of the last few days, Frank supposed it was possible for Stevens to forget. Still, it seemed strange. Could Stevens be planning another publicity stunt?

"How many people had access to the original disks?" Frank asked.

"They weren't locked up. Anyone could have taken them," Stevens said. "But it wasn't someone in this house—these people are my friends." Stevens stopped pacing and crossed his arms in front of his chest.

"We have one other lead I'd like to follow up on," Joe said. "Deke Ramsey. He threatened you. He may have decided to act on his threat."

"Or have his son do it," Frank added.

"I don't see how Deke Ramsey can be involved with what's happening here." Stevens shook his head. "Still, maybe you should talk to him—if you can find him."

"Ramsey said he was writing a book," Frank

recalled. "Would he have an agent or publisher working with him?"

"Probably," Stevens replied. "I could ask the Lip. The hospital is going to release him later today."

"That's good news. We could try your publicist, too," Joe suggested.

"Good idea." Stevens reached for the telephone. "Joyce has connections throughout the industry. If anyone can find Ramsey, she can."

After hanging up, Stevens told the Hardys that his publicist wanted to meet with them at a restaurant in town. Two hours later Joe and Frank walked into the Ashfork Steak Works, which was located on the ground level of a large glass-and-steel building. A hostess escorted the Hardys to Joyce's table.

"Thanks for seeing us," Frank said as Joyce shook hands with them.

"No problem," she replied. "After Mark explained the situation, I knew we couldn't meet at his house. And after talking with him, I was eager to see you two again."

"Why?" Joe asked.

Joyce sat down. "I could really do something with you guys. A newspaper piece, magazine articles, maybe a TV spot. A pair of handsome teenage hawkshaws—you're a publicist's dream!"

"Hawkshaws?" Frank asked, amused.

"Private investigators," she explained.

"You couldn't mention our current case," Joe said. "We wouldn't want to blow our cover."

Joyce's enthusiasm drained away. "You're right. Mark told me to keep a lid on everything."

If Stevens was behind this and wanted publicity, he'd have let Joyce notify the press about what was happening, Frank thought. "How long have you worked for him?" he asked.

"From the beginning," Joyce said. "He's one of my best clients. But he didn't hire me initially. His agent did."

"Robert Lipp?" Joe asked.

"Yes." Joyce sighed. "Years ago Lipp was Deke Ramsey's agent. He and Ramsey had a falling out, and Lipp was fired."

Joe thought he knew where the story was going. "But then he found Mark Stevens."

Joyce nodded. "Stevens and Ramsey wrote the same type of books. To give his new client an edge, Lipp hired my firm to come up with a publicity stunt for his first book."

Joyce waved away an approaching waitress. Leaning over the table, she said, "The stunt wasn't much—we dressed some bikers up like zombies and had them crash a society party. It made all the papers. *Colors of the Dead* was a big hit."

"Was Ramsey jealous?" Frank asked.

"Oh, my, yes. His career sank after that. It was rumored that Robert Lipp had given Ramsey all his book ideas." Joyce sighed. "It can't be true because if it were, Ramsey would never have fired Lipp. Still, Ramsey hasn't had a successful book since."

Pressing her fingertips together thoughtfully, Joyce studied the Hardys. "Am I a suspect in Mark's troubles?"

"Not exactly a suspect . . ." Joe hedged.

She laughed briefly. "Good. If I were, I'd have an alibi. I was in Europe when all the problems started. And, yes, I can prove it."

"Someone else in your office might have seen the novel outline," Frank said.

"Never. Mark would scalp me if I didn't keep it to myself." Joyce passed a slip of paper over the table. "I found Deke Ramsey's address for you. If you're looking for a bad guy, he's my candidate. But be careful. He's dangerous."

After leaving the restaurant, Frank and Joe returned to the van and looked at the slip of paper Joyce had given them.

"We passed Ramsey's street on the way over here. We can be there in twenty minutes, tops," Joe said. A little while later Joe pulled the van to a stop in front of a building.

"We must have gotten the address wrong," Frank said.

Joe showed him the paper. "Seventeen-fifty Kent Way."

"Nobody lives in a bookstore." Resting his

chin in his hand, Frank peered at the building across the street. It had a sign painted on its plate-glass window: All Paperbacks 50% Off!

Joe opened the driver's door. "Ramsey might have his mail delivered here. Let's find out."

A bell tinkled as they entered the shop. Joe stood in the entrance, near the racks of paperback books. Straight ahead, he saw that large metal-framed bookcases had been set up back to back to form aisles. There weren't any customers in the store.

"Joe," Frank said softly. "This place is more than Ramsey's mail drop."

Frank pointed to the far end of the store, where Deke Ramsey was standing beside a cash register. He was turned so his profile was to them as he put a roll of quarters in the change drawer.

Ramsey raised his head, and his eyes widened as he recognized the Hardys. "You!"

Frank and Joe advanced slowly. "We just want to talk," Joe said.

Ramsey backed away from them, bolting suddenly for the rear exit behind the cash register counter.

Frank and Joe sprinted after him. As they rushed forward, Frank caught a glimpse of a familiar person as he ducked down. Carl Ramsey was now crouching near the back door, hiding behind a bookcase.

"Watch it!" Frank cried to his brother.

It was too late. Lurching to his feet, Carl shoved against the freestanding bookcase. The bookcase teetered and fell, sending hundreds of books crashing down toward the Hardys.

Chapter

9

FRANK THREW himself sideways, rolling as he hit the floor. He snugged up against the sales counter, shielding his head from the books raining down on him.

The last couple of volumes thumped to the ground, stirring up tiny puffs of dust. Frank raised his head over the counter. "Joe?"

"Over here." Joe pulled himself out from under a display table of mystery novels. The table had been rocked by the deadly avalanche but had remained upright.

Joe brushed back his tousled hair. "Let's get 'em," he said with fire in his eyes.

Rushing outside, the Hardys saw Carl Ramsey standing alone in the back parking lot. As Joe started across the blacktop, he heard the roar of a car engine. With its tires squealing, Ramsey's old convertible fishtailed into the lot. The passenger door popped open, and Carl jumped in beside his father. Trailing a stream of exhaust, the convertible raced away.

"Come on!" Joe cried. "Let's go out front and get the van."

Frank watched as the convertible bucked onto the road, narrowly avoiding a collision. "Let them go," he said.

"Let them go?" Joe exclaimed. "We can catch that piece of junk!"

"I know we can," Frank said. "But Ramsey won't talk to us now, no matter what. So why chase him? We've got better things to do."

"Like what?" Joe asked, frustrated.

"I thought I'd shop for a new book."

"Shop?" Joe said. "Now?"

Frank grinned. Turning, he walked back inside the bookstore.

Then Joe understood—Ramsey had left the store open and unlocked. It was the perfect opportunity to search for any clues he might have left behind. "I'm right behind you!" he called.

Back inside, they found that the building was still deserted. Frank bolted the front door and put a Closed sign in the window. "We'll leave through the back," he said.

From the other side of the shop, Joe whistled softly. "Look at this."

Joe was standing in a corner of the store, facing a display of horror novels. The centerpiece of the display was a rack that held nothing but used copies of Deke Ramsey books. A hand-lettered sign above the rack promised that a new Deke Ramsey novel would be out soon.

Joe was flipping through a volume when Frank joined him. "Ramsey's last book came out almost four years ago," Joe said.

"I wonder what he's been doing since then," Frank said. "It's kind of sad, really. Did you notice there's not one novel by Mark Stevens here?"

"That's no surprise."

Frank walked over to a wooden desk and opened the top drawer. Inside, he found a small silver picture frame.

"What's that?" Joe asked.

Frank picked up the picture. "It looks like an old photograph."

Joe took the picture. In the photograph a dark-haired Deke Ramsey had his arm around a smiling woman. A boy and a girl were standing in front of them. Ramsey and the children shared the same startlingly gray eyes.

"Looks like a family photo," Joe said.

Frank's reply was cut off by a loud shriek that echoed throughout the shop. "What have you done to my store?" a voice demanded.

A well-dressed, curly-haired woman had entered through the back door. Her round face was flushed in outrage. "Look at this—this—mess!"

she sputtered. She wildly waved an arm, bringing it under control to gesture at the damage.

The fallen bookcase lay in front of her, blocking the aisle. Books were scattered everywhere.

"Who are you?" Frank asked.

"I'm Judy Woods, the store's owner. I step out for fifteen minutes—" She shook her head angrily. "I'm calling the police."

"You don't need to do that," Joe hastily assured her. "We can explain—I hope."

At their explanation, Judy's anger slowly faded. "I should have known," she said. "Ramsey and his no-good son have been nothing but trouble for me. Coming in late, closing early—I should have fired them a long time ago."

"Why didn't you?" Frank asked.

Judy's eyes softened. "I felt sorry for Ramsey, I guess. He was a writer, once. I've always had a soft spot for writers."

"Why was he working here?" Joe asked.

"He needed a job," Judy said flatly. She glanced at the photo in Joe's hand. "After Ramsey's writing career crumbled, his wife divorced him. She took the kids with her."

"But his son came back," Frank said.

"About eighteen months ago," she told them. "The boy's just more bad luck, if you ask me."

Joe replaced the picture frame. "Do you have Ramsey's current address?"

A glint of surprise showed in the storeowner's eyes. "You don't know it?"

"No," Joe admitted.

Judy slowly smiled. "I'll make a trade with you," she said. "Ramsey's address for your help in cleaning up my store."

"But—" Frank started to protest. It would take an hour to clean up the mess.

"We'll have it done in no time," Judy said reassuringly. "Is it a deal?"

Frank sighed. "It's a deal."

Working together, Joe and Frank lifted the bookcase back into position. With Judy's help they restocked it. Once everything was done, she thanked them warmly.

"The address?" Joe asked.

"You've earned it." With a trace of embarrassment, Judy said, "Seventeen-fifty Kent Way."

"But that's this address!" Frank said.

"There's an apartment over the store. I rent it to the Ramseys." She blushed. "I know it was a dirty trick, but I needed your help. I'll pay you for your time."

"It was no trouble," Joe said.

Frank was struck by a sudden thought. "Give us some information, instead," he said. "Do you know if Ramsey uses a manual typewriter?"

"I couldn't say. Is it important?"

"It might be," Frank told her.

Judy opened her purse, pulling out a ring of keys. "Here. I owe you," she said. "You can go up to the apartment to see for yourself. But don't touch anything!"

Frank and Joe followed her through a side storage area and up a flight of stairs. They waited as she sorted through her keys before opening the door to Ramsey's apartment.

Joe could smell musty air inside. A sofa bed was folded out in the living room, the sheets in a tangled heap. Old newspapers littered the floor beneath it. An empty pizza box, stained with grease, sat on the coffee table.

"It's a pigsty!" Judy said, dismayed. Forgetting about Joe and Frank, she hurried inside to investigate the kitchen.

"I'll check the bedroom," Joe said. Frank took the living room. He found a newspaper that had listed the date for Mark Stevens's lecture at the Ashfork Playhouse. The announcement had been circled in red ink.

Joe came to the bedroom doorway. "Check out what I just found," he told Frank.

Inside the room Frank walked around an unmade double bed to join his brother. Joe was bent over a metal desk. A typewriter sat on the desk top.

"It's electric," Joe said before Frank could ask. "But take a look at this."

Beside the typewriter was a stack of paper. Frank picked up the cover sheet. "It's the outline for Ramsey's novel."

"Read the first page," Joe suggested.

Frank scanned it. With growing interest he

read it again. Quickly he flipped through the next few pages of the outline. "I can't believe it."

"It's all there," Joe said. "The shattered mirrors, the dying flowers, the tombstone in the garden. Someone falls downstairs, there are voices in the night, poisonings. It's not a duplicate of Stevens's work, but it's so close it won't matter."

"Ramsey must have seen Mark's outline," Frank said. "But how?"

"He stole it—or someone gave it to him," Joe replied. "But it doesn't make sense. Ramsey must know he'd never get away with it."

"Maybe he thinks it's owed to him," Frank remarked. "That's essentially what he said at the Playhouse. He said Stevens had used his idea for a book, and he was bent on getting revenge."

"Some revenge," Joe said.

Going into the bedroom, Judy Woods took the pages from Frank. "You weren't supposed to touch anything," she scolded. After returning the sheets to the desk, she escorted the Hardys out of the apartment.

Frank and Joe left Judy at the bookstore. Outside, they crossed the street to their van. "Mark Stevens needs to know about this," Frank said.

"Let's go back to the house," Joe agreed.

As they neared their van, a man moved out from the back of the vehicle. He was in his midthirties, Joe guessed, with hair that had been shaved down to blond nubs. This guy looks like an army sergeant, Joe thought.

"Frank and Joe Hardy?" The man stepped in front of them.

"Yes," Frank replied warily. He couldn't help noticing that the stranger had a massive build. His lightweight warm-up jacket couldn't hide the muscles that bulged beneath its fabric.

"Good," the man said. "I wouldn't want to make a mistake." Reaching behind his back, he pulled something from his waistband. When his hand reappeared, it was holding a gun.

Frank drew back. The gun's shape was familiar. It was an Uzi semiautomatic pistol, one of the deadliest weapons made.

Joe recognized it, too. "Take it easy," he said. "You don't need a gun. If there's a problem, we can talk about it."

A slow smile crossed the stranger's face. "I don't have a problem," he said. "*You* have the problem. You're messing with things that don't concern you. I'm here to put a stop to it."

He raised the pistol, pointing it at Joe. His finger tightened around the trigger.

"Don't!" Frank shouted, charging the man.

The stranger swung around, leveled his gun arm at Frank, and pulled the pistol's trigger.

Wummmpf! The gun fired. Frank jerked back as he was struck in the chest. He stumbled, falling to the ground.

Frank rolled onto his back as a bright red stain spread across the front of his shirt.

Chapter

10

"FRANK!" Joe cried, kneeling beside his brother.

Frank sat upright. He'd felt a blow when the gun fired, but it hadn't hurt.

"I'm okay," he told his brother. "It's only paint," he said, rubbing his fingers over the stain.

"Consider this a warning," the stranger said, looking down on them. "Next time I'll use real bullets."

He raised his pistol. Firing it repeatedly, he sent a volley of paint pellets at the van. Joe protected his eyes from the splattering missiles that coated his shirt and pants.

When he lifted his head, Joe saw the man running down the sidewalk. Scrambling to his feet, Joe took off after him.

Joe followed the stranger and saw him stop beside an unoccupied pickup truck.

With a frantic burst of speed, Joe caught up with him. He yanked him around and then grabbed at the front of his warm-up jacket. "Hold it!" Joe shouted.

The stranger's warm-up jacket pulled open. Joe caught a glimpse of the tank top beneath it. The design on the shirt was of a muscular figure standing between two stone pillars.

The man seemed surprised by Joe's sudden appearance. "You've got guts, pal," he said. "I'll give you that."

With a powerful shove the stranger sent Joe sprawling to the asphalt. The man climbed into the pickup and drove away.

Frank ran up behind his brother. "What were you going to do once you caught him?" he asked. "Beat him up?"

Joe grinned. "That was my plan. Did you get his license number?"

Frank helped Joe to his feet. "I couldn't read it. There was mud on both plates."

"Why did I expect that?" Joe started to brush himself off but gave up in disgust. Between the dirt and the paint, he'd never get clean. "Who was that guy, anyway? What does he have to do with Stevens?"

"Whoever sent him after us had to know where we were," Frank stated.

"Joyce knew," Joe said as they walked back to the van. "Ramsey did, too."

"It couldn't have been Ramsey," Frank said. "If he had a friend like that, he'd never have sent his son to follow me."

"Maybe his friend wasn't available." Joe grimaced when he saw the paint-smeared van ahead of them. "I hope that stuff comes off," he said.

After stopping at a car wash, the Hardys returned to Nightmare House with a relatively clean car. Michelle met them at the front door, taking in their paint-stained clothes. "My goodness," she said. "What happened to you?"

The alarm in her eyes caused Frank to give his clothing a fresh glance. He and Joe did look like survivors of a paint-store explosion. "It's hard to explain."

"Wait here." Leaving them in the entryway, Michelle hurried out.

When she returned, she had two robes draped over one arm. In her free hand she carried two large plastic bags. "After you've cleaned up, put your clothing in the bags. I'll take care of it."

"Thanks," Frank said, accepting a robe and bag. "Is Callie around?"

"She's upstairs in the office," Michelle replied. "Working."

"What about Mr. Stevens?" Joe asked.

"He's working, too," Michelle said, sounding pleased. "He's writing again."

"We need to talk to him," Joe told her.

Michelle shook her head. "Mr. Stevens can't be disturbed when he's writing. It's the house rule. He won't see anyone."

Frank moved toward the stairs. "We'll talk to him when he's done, then."

"It could be a while," she said. "He often writes through the night. Is it something Mr. Lipp can help you with? He's back from the hospital and resting upstairs."

Michelle handed Joe a robe as he followed Frank up to their bedroom.

Joe opened the door. "Do we tell Lipp?"

"He needs to know about Ramsey's outline," Frank said. "As Stevens's agent, he can take the necessary steps to protect his client's work."

After a shower and a change of clothes, Frank and Joe went to Lipp's room. The agent invited them in. He was lying in bed, reading. Although he was still pale, he was obviously much better.

The room was almost identical to Callie's, with a double bed, dresser, and nightstand. But Frank knew Lipp's closet didn't have a secret passage behind it.

"I guess I gave everyone a bit of a scare yesterday," the agent said somewhat sheepishly. "The doctors couldn't find anything wrong except that my blood pressure was very low, which would account for my fainting."

"The water did taste bitter, though. It's a good thing I spit it out right away," he added grimly. "If I'd swallowed, who knows what might have happened. We've got to find out who's behind all this before someone really is killed!"

Lipp listened as the Hardys told him about their discovery in Ramsey's apartment. "How could Deke Ramsey have seen one of Mark's outlines?" Lipp asked, perplexed.

"We don't know," Frank admitted.

"There's always a way, I suppose," Lipp said. "He could have asked a friend at the publishing house. Maybe Joyce got careless—or Bev."

"What are you going to do to protect Mark's work now?" Joe asked.

"I'll start by contacting our attorney," he replied. "He might suggest we go to the police. We'll see."

From downstairs they heard the tinkling of the dinner bell. "I thought Mark made a mistake bringing you here," Lipp told them. "I was wrong. You've solved the mystery."

"We still don't have all the answers," Frank cautioned. "There's no evidence that Ramsey was ever at Nightmare House."

"But—surely you're satisfied that he's behind all of this? It makes perfect sense."

"It looks that way," Frank agreed. Joe and Frank's father, Fenton Hardy, had always warned them about making assumptions. Without solid proof Ramsey's guilt was only that—a king-size assumption.

"Well, *I'm* convinced," Lipp declared. "And I know that Mark will be, too."

Stevens remained in his office during dinner, and Michelle carried a tray of food to Lipp's room. Only Bev ate in the dining room with Callie and the Hardys. After supper was finished, Bev quickly left the room.

When Michelle stepped into the kitchen, Frank asked Callie how her day had gone.

"I'm a flop as a detective," Callie said unhappily.

It was an opening for an easy gibe, but Joe didn't take it. One look at Callie's face told him that she wasn't in the mood to be teased. "What happened?" he asked.

"You wanted that file on Mark's first hit book," she answered. "I found it, but I couldn't take it. Bev watched me constantly. If I dared touch anything that wasn't a fan letter, she had a fit!"

"I'd like to see that file," Frank said. "Stevens's notes might tell us if, perhaps, he got the book idea from Ramsey."

"Or if Lipp did," Joe pointed out. "Why don't we go up to the study now?" he said in a low voice.

"Everything's locked up," Callie whispered.

"Bev is probably lurking in the hallway, watching for us."

"She's not very trusting," Frank said.

"I think she's heard or figured out that you're detectives. I heard her mumble something about a pair of snoops."

"So much for our cover." Joe looked at Callie. "What are you going to do next?"

Callie's jaw was stubbornly set. "I'm going to get that file."

At breakfast the next morning, Stevens was still working. Robert Lipp, however, came downstairs and joined the others at the table. "Mark says that things are going wonderfully," he said in a bright voice.

Michelle leaned over to pour him a cup of coffee. He held his hand up to stop her. "Not today," he said. "With news like this—perhaps champagne?"

Michelle responded with a gentle smile. "Dr. Gilbreth wouldn't approve," she said. "You have another appointment this afternoon."

"It's only a routine checkup," Lipp protested. "Well—later, then."

He beamed happily. Lipp's rare display of high spirits was enough to brighten everyone's mood.

After breakfast Joe asked Michelle for a telephone directory, which he took back to his bedroom.

"Found it," he said with satisfaction.

Frank came over to him. "What?"

Joe turned the directory so that Frank could see it. "When Muscles was tossing me around yesterday, I caught a look at his T-shirt. There was a drawing on it."

Joe stabbed a finger at an advertisement under the listing for health clubs. "The drawing on this ad matches the one on his shirt."

" 'Samson's Fitness Center,' " Frank read.

"Located in beautiful downtown Ashfork," Joe said, closing the directory. "I'll get the van keys."

It was midmorning when they pulled into the parking lot of the gym. Frank was impressed with the size of the building and its handsome redwood exterior. Although it was a weekday, the parking lot was full. Through the front windows of the gym, he could see an aerobics class in session.

Inside the building Frank and Joe stopped at the front desk. The dark-haired girl behind the counter perked up as they entered. "New members, right?" She gave Joe a dazzling smile. "I'd remember if I'd seen you before."

"We're not members," Frank said. "We're trying to find somebody."

"Oh? Animal or human?" She grinned at their puzzled expressions. "The humans do aerobics, use the Nautilus, and have a life. The animals are big and beefy. They don't do anything but pump iron."

"Animal—I guess," Joe said, chuckling.

"Go to your left, into the weight room. Ask for Ralph." She rested a hand on Joe's arm. "If you do decide to become a member, I'd *love* to talk to you."

Joe smiled back at the girl.

"You're incredible, Joe," Frank quipped. "The human magnet strikes again."

"Why couldn't Bev be like her?" Joe asked, laughing as they crossed the carpeted floor.

Entering the weight room, they were greeted by the clanking of iron weights and the smell of sweat. Most of the people in the room were male. Many of them wore tank tops or T-shirts with the gym's logo on it.

A barrel-chested man with thinning hair came up to the Hardys. "Can I help you?"

"We're looking for Ralph," Frank said.

"That's me. I'm the floor supervisor."

"We're trying to locate somebody," Joe told him. "We think he's a member of your gym."

Ralph listened to Joe's description of the man that had ambushed them. When he was done, Ralph nodded. "Sounds like you want Mac McCoy," he said. "Bad Mac McCoy, they call him."

At McCoy's name, Frank noticed a pair of bodybuilders drift closer. The first man was short and dark skinned, with tattoos on both arms. The other man was taller, with a fair complexion. His long, stringy hair was pulled into a ponytail that hung down his back.

Ralph waved them away. "Back off, guys. This doesn't concern you."

Reluctantly they turned away. "Where can we find McCoy?" Frank asked.

"Not here," Ralph answered. "Mac has a hot temper and a short fuse. He's been banned from the club."

"We need to locate him," Joe pressed.

Ralph shrugged. "Sorry. His membership card was pulled when he got kicked out."

The two bodybuilders had remained close by. Ralph guided the Hardys away from them. "I might have one lead. McCoy is a war-gamer. He and his pals have weekend fantasy battles over at Watkins Ridge. They dress up in camouflage outfits and shoot each other with paint balloons. Their guns look incredibly realistic."

"A war-gamer!" Joe said. "Of course."

Peering over his shoulder, Frank saw that the two bodybuilders were leaving. They were walking out of the weight room toward the front desk.

As Frank turned back, Ralph said, "I'd suggest you stay away from Bad Mac. The word is, he's for hire. He's a high-priced leg-breaker—and he likes his work."

After thanking him, Frank and Joe left the gym. "Ramsey doesn't have a dime to spare,"

Frank said. "He couldn't afford to hire someone like Bad Mac McCoy."

Joe stopped walking. "Trouble ahead."

The two bodybuilders from the weight room were in the parking lot, watching them. They leaned against a car parked near the entrance.

"That's why they left early," Frank said. "They wanted to catch us outside."

The short bodybuilder smiled at them, a shiny gold tooth flashing from inside his mouth. "We been waiting for you," he told the Hardys. "We heard you asking questions about our buddy, Mac McCoy."

Joe took a step to his left. As he expected, the shorter man quickly jumped up and blocked his path.

At close range Joe examined the man. This isn't going to be easy, he thought. Even his muscles have muscles.

The tall bodybuilder walked over to Frank. "Mac's in a sensitive line of business," the tall man said. "He doesn't like questions. Questions stir up trouble. They can get somebody hurt."

He raised a fist. "Somebody like you."

Chapter

11

FRANK TOOK a step backward. This is going to be like fighting King Kong, he thought.

Joe's opponent was smaller but had the same powerful physique. The bodybuilder poked his finger into Joe's chest. "Come on, punk," he said. "Show me what you've got. Take your best shot."

The bodybuilder raised his tattooed arms, exposing a stomach that was ridged with muscle. "Or are you afraid?" he asked in a cocky tone of voice. The bodybuilder was so sure that he couldn't be hurt that he was daring Joe to hit him.

"You asked for it," Joe said. He swung, driving his left fist into the muscled abdomen. His knuckles stung as they hit. He felt as if he'd punched a brick wall!

The bodybuilder shrugged off the blow. "That was it?" he said with a smirk. "That was your best shot?"

"No," Joe said. He sent his right fist smashing against the man's chin.

The punch jolted the man, knocking him from his feet. He lay on the ground, stunned.

"*That* was my best shot," Joe said.

The other bodybuilder didn't wait. He swung at Frank. His large right hand punched only air, missing its target by inches.

As he dodged the punch, Frank got ready and whirled into a spinning kick. His foot slammed into his opponent's ribs. The bodybuilder folded up like an accordion.

Behind them the front door of the gym creaked open. Ralph came into the parking lot and bellowed, "That's enough!"

Joe and Frank stepped back from their attackers. With help from his friend the short man got to his feet. "I'm gonna stomp—"

Ralph cut him off. "It's over, Greco. You know the rules—no fighting. You and Tommy get your gear and get out of here."

Grumbling, the bodybuilders backed away. Muttering vague threats, they went inside the gym.

"After they get their stuff from the locker room, they'll be back out," Ralph said. "I'd appreciate it if you two were gone by then."

"So would I," Frank replied.

"Don't worry," Joe said. "We're out of here."

"One other favor," Ralph added. "Stay away from my club. We don't like trouble here. And anyone looking for Bad Mac McCoy is nothing but trouble."

When the Hardys returned to the mansion, Frank saw that Lipp's car was gone from the driveway. Bev's small sports car was missing, too. "Where is everybody?" he asked.

"Lipp went to see the doctor," Joe reminded him. "And who cares where Bev is? The longer she's gone, the better."

Going into the house, Frank and Joe found Callie waiting for them. "I'm glad you're here," she said. "Come up to my room."

They went up the stairs. Once inside the bedroom Joe asked, "Where's your keeper?"

"Bev used the noon break to run into town. She said she had some personal errands." Callie wrinkled her nose. "She locked every cabinet and drawer before she left."

Callie went to the maple dresser in her closet and pulled a white folder from the middle drawer. "Ta-dah!"

Frank took the folder from her. *Colors of the Dead* was written across the upper tab.

"It's the information on Mark's first big book," Callie said with pride.

"How did you get it?" Frank asked.

"After breakfast Stevens paged Bev to come to his office. She was only gone a minute." There was a glow of triumph on Callie's face. "That was plenty of time. I took it from the file cabinet and buried it under the fan mail. When Bev locked up, I already had it."

Frank opened the folder. It held several pages of handwritten notes, as well as a number of newspaper clippings about inner-city gangs. There were also a few letters enclosed, mostly from Stevens's publisher and Robert Lipp.

Callie continued speaking. "I didn't know when you'd be back, so, when Bev left, I tried to find a place to hide the folder. I decided to slip it between the mattress and the box spring of my bed."

"Not a bad idea," Joe said. "Why didn't you put it there?"

"Because something else was there." Lifting the bedcover, Callie brought out a pair of unlabeled computer disks. "I think these might be Mark's missing computer disks."

Frank took the disks from Callie. "They're not labeled," he said.

"There's a computer in Bev's office," Joe said. "We could see what's on them."

"Good idea." Frank returned the folder to Callie's dresser. "We'll save that for later. Let's find out what's on these disks."

The trio quickly made their way to the study.

Joe cracked the door open and peered inside. "All clear."

The computer sat on Bev's desk. Sliding into her chair, Frank pulled the keyboard forward. After switching on the machine, he put the disks in their separate drives.

When a cursor appeared on the monitor, Frank entered a standard command. To his relief, the computer responded. It brought up a directory of the stored files.

"We're in," Frank said. He scrolled through the files, looking for a starting point.

Callie pointed at the screen. "Try that one."

Frank called up the listing for Book IX.

The monitor's display changed. "That's it," Joe said. "Book nine is Stevens's new novel."

"Someone must have planted the disks in my room," Callie said.

"And it wouldn't surprise me if that someone was Bev," Frank said. He brought the directory back on screen.

"See if you can find the book's outline," Callie requested. "I haven't seen it yet."

With a few fast strokes Frank brought it up. " 'Chapter One—The Screaming Dead,' " he read aloud. " 'Chapter Two—A River of Blood.' "

Callie made a face. "Are all of Mark's books like this?" she asked.

"More or less," Joe replied.

"How can you stand to read them?" Callie asked.

Joe raised a warning finger to his lips. "Someone's coming," he said in a hushed voice.

Listening, Frank heard footsteps. Someone was walking toward the office.

He quickly retrieved the two computer disks. Passing them to Callie, he turned off the machine. The computer screen went blank.

After hurrying to her own desk, Callie dropped the disks into a box of oversized envelopes. She was closing the lid when the door swung open.

Bev came in. When she saw the Hardys in the room, her eyes narrowed. "Why are you in here?" she demanded. She glared at Frank suspiciously. "What are you doing at my desk?"

Frank cleared his throat. "Is this your desk?" He lifted himself out of the chair. "I didn't know."

"We were just talking," Callie told her. "After all, this is my break, too."

Bev studied her. "Break's over. Tell your friends to leave. We have work to do."

"It's okay," Joe said. "We were going anyway."

Suddenly a tinny voice called over the intercom, "Bev, are you in there? Callie?"

Frank recognized the frightened voice. It was Stevens's.

"If anyone can hear me, help me!" the writer cried. "Hurry!"

Callie pressed the intercom button. "Mr. Stevens? We don't know where you are." When there wasn't an answer, she asked urgently, "Which room are you in?"

The only reply was a crackle of static.

"You just came from downstairs," Joe told Bev. "Was Stevens there?"

"I didn't see him," she answered.

"He must be in his office or his bedroom," Frank said. "Let's try the office first." Like Bev's office, it was on the second floor. If it was empty, they could race up to his bedroom in seconds.

Frank and Joe ran from Bev's office, Callie and Bev following, trying to keep up.

Stevens's office door was closed when they reached it. Frank turned the knob, and the door swung open.

Inside, Mark Stevens was cowering against the far wall. The intercom buzzed with static, just beyond his reach.

"Be careful," Stevens said in a strangled voice.

Joe stepped into the room behind Frank. He couldn't believe the scene that met his eyes.

One of the desk drawers had fallen to the ground. Two large green-and-brown snakes were coiled up inside it, their tongues flicking in and out nervously. A third snake had slithered out of the drawer and was moving toward Stevens.

The writer was shaking with fright.

Standing behind Frank and Joe, Callie asked, "What's going on?"

Joe stepped aside, letting Callie and Bev come in from the hallway. When she saw the snakes, Bev gave a startled gasp.

Callie was stunned. "Poisonous vipers," she said. "Just like in the outline."

Chapter

12

FRANK QUICKLY surveyed the room. Beside the door was a small wicker container filled with trash. "Give me that wastebasket," he said.

Joe took the basket and dumped its contents on the ground before passing it to his brother.

Holding the basket in one hand, Frank slowly approached the reptiles. Out of the corner of one eye, he could see Bev shrinking against the wall, her face pale with fright.

"Don't get too close," Callie said. "They're dangerous!"

"Dangerous? To a gopher, maybe." Frank inched closer, moving toward the fallen drawer. "These snakes aren't vipers; they're garden snakes. Joe and I see them when we go camping."

Taking a closer look, Joe realized that Frank was right. Snakes weren't common in the woods around Bayport, but there were always a few to be found. They'd glide across the fallen leaves or wriggle down rodent holes.

Interesting, Joe thought. He knew that war-gamers loved to have their battles among trees. Did Bad Mac McCoy take time out from his games to do a little reptile collecting?

As the others watched Frank creep toward the snakes, Joe silently slipped out of the room.

He was confident that Frank could handle the situation in Stevens's office. With Bev preoccupied, it was the perfect opportunity for him to return to her office. He could safely collect the computer disks that Callie had left behind.

Joe slipped inside the room and closed the door. He opened the box of envelopes and plucked out the two computer disks.

Joe let his eyes roam over the filing cabinets and the secretary's desk. The only sign of clutter was the pile of letters on Callie's desk. Everything else was in its place. Even Bev's desk was perfectly neat.

Did Bev really think Callie was a thief? Joe asked himself. Or was Bev hiding a secret of her own?

Returning to the door, Joe checked out the hallway. There was no one in sight. He could hear vacuuming from the lower floor, a sure sign that Michelle wouldn't interrupt him.

Unless Lipp made an unexpected appearance, Joe was alone. He looked at his wristwatch. He'd give himself five minutes to go over the room. After that, he'd have to leave.

Joe went over to the filing cabinets. They were sturdy, constructed of heavy steel. Putting the computer disks on top of them, Joe pulled at the upper drawers. They wouldn't budge. Given enough time and the proper tools, he was certain he could pick the simple locks that closed them.

"No tools," he said to himself. "No time." The minutes were ticking away.

Keeping the disks with him, he knelt beside Bev's desk. It was made of oak and brass and had its own lock. Joe tugged at the decorative handles, trying to free a drawer.

The bottom right-hand drawer wriggled when he pulled it. It slid forward, revealing a tiny part of its metal catch. There wasn't much of an opening. The gap was less than a half-inch wide.

It would have to do. Joe raised his head over the desk, looking for something small enough to slide into the opening. A paper clip, maybe, or a letter opener—

A letter opener! There was one on Callie's desk, next to the pile of mail.

After snatching the letter opener, Joe bent back over the drawer. He pressed the tip of the letter opener against the catch, trying to force it to release the drawer. The catch dropped suddenly, springing the lock.

Joe quickly pulled out the drawer.

It was nearly empty. It held a stack of white paper and, beneath that, a women's fashion magazine.

Joe surveyed the contents with a frown. "Why did I bother?" he said quietly

Putting the magazine aside, he leafed through the paper. It was a good-quality typing paper—nothing out of the ordinary. As Stevens's secretary, Bev must have used it regularly.

A glance at his watch told Joe that his five minutes were up. Time to go.

A noise from the hallway made Joe freeze in place. Someone was just outside the door! Peering over the desk, Joe saw the doorknob turning.

Ducking down, he put the computer disks at the bottom of the drawer. He heard the office door open as he placed the stack of paper on top of the disks. Quietly Joe pushed the drawer closed.

Too late he realized he hadn't put the magazine away. Curling it into a cylinder, Joe gripped it like a weapon. Cautiously he raised up from the desk.

Bev was in front of him on the opposite side of the desk. When she saw Joe, she raised her hand to her mouth in surprise.

No, Joe thought. Not *her*.

As Bev recovered from her shock, a furious scowl appeared on her face. Moving in closer toward the desk, she faltered. As quickly as it had come, her scowl faded.

"Oh, Joe," she murmured, stepping still closer. To his astonishment, she smiled at him and reached over and put a hand on his arm.

Joe gulped. "Bev?"

"I'm sorry for the way I've been acting," Bev cooed. "I know I've been snappish and short-tempered. It's because there's been so much tension in this house. I'm not usually like that, honest."

Bev was so close he could smell the perfume she was wearing. "That's all right," Joe said.

"No, it isn't." She met Joe's eyes. "It's wrong. I hope you'll forgive me." She took his hand in hers.

"Consider yourself forgiven." He pulled away from her.

Bev looked hurt. "I'd like to be friends—if you'll let me."

"Sure." He edged around to the side of the desk and away from her. As affectionate as Bev was pretending to be, Joe wasn't buying it. He'd seen her real personality, and it was nothing like this.

Bev was as warm and friendly as a shark.

"Don't go," she said softly.

"I'd better let you get back to work." Joe scooted out the door and moved into the hallway, pulling the door closed behind him.

He was still standing in the hallway, a stunned

expression on his face, when Frank and Callie joined him in the hall. "So there you are," Frank said. "You look like you just saw a ghost."

"Anything is possible around here," Joe said. "What happened to the snakes?"

"We herded them into the wastebasket," Callie replied. "Then Frank released them into Mr. Stevens's garden."

"Gophers beware." Glancing toward Bev's office door, Frank dropped his voice. "What's up?"

"While you were busy, I decided to collect the computer disks," Joe said.

"Did you get them?" Frank asked.

"Not exactly." Moving farther down the hall, Joe explained what had happened.

"They're in Bev's desk?" Callie asked in alarm.

"Under a ream of typing paper," Joe said. "Don't worry, I'll get them back." He remembered the magazine in his hand. Loosening his grip, he let it uncurl. "This was in the desk, too. I'll have to return it."

Frank took it from him. "Got tired of sports magazines?"

"Very funny," Joe said, batting Frank on the arm with the magazine.

Squatting, Callie picked a glossy page from the floor. "This fell out of your magazine."

"It's not *my* magazine," Joe said.

Callie lifted the loose page for the others to see. "You wouldn't want it, anyway. It's been cut up."

"Cut up?" Frank repeated. A closer glance told him that Callie was right. There was a rectangular hole in the page.

Frank flipped through the magazine. It was missing more than the one page. Letters and words had been cut out of its different sections. "Joe—" he began.

"I see it," Joe said in a tight voice. "Now I know why Bev was acting so weird. She noticed the magazine in my hand and wanted it back, but she couldn't demand it because that would look too suspicious. So she decided to try a little sweet talk instead."

Callie looked from one brother to the other. "What are you talking about?"

"Bev cut up the magazine," Frank told her. "She used the different letters to spell out a string of words. She wanted to leave a message that couldn't be easily traced."

"A message? What kind of message?" Callie asked.

"A death threat," Joe said. "The one she left in Stevens's office that read, 'I will cut out your heart.' "

"Why would Bev leave Stevens a death threat?" Callie asked.

"Let's ask her." Going to the office door, Frank gripped the doorknob. It wouldn't turn.

"It locks from the inside," Callie explained. "There isn't a key." She knocked at the door. "Bev. It's Callie. Let me in."

There was no answer.

Joe sniffed at the air. "I smell something burning."

Frank tried the handle again, shaking it and banging on the door. "This door's hot!" he exclaimed.

"There's a fire!" Callie shrieked. She pointed to the bottom of the door. Frank and Joe saw smoke pouring out and growing thicker by the second.

"Interior doors are usually hollow!" Joe cried. "I'll bet this one is, too."

"Go for it," Frank told his brother.

Jumping up, Joe kicked the door, putting all his weight behind it.

The door cracked on impact. A second kick broke the lock. The door swung open.

Bev was gone. The curtains at the windows were all in flames!

Chapter

13

JOE MOVED quickly into the room. He grabbed the edge of the heavy area rug and yanked it up from the floor, overturning several chairs.

"Help me smother the flames!" he shouted.

Frank had already grabbed the other side of the carpet. The Hardys held it in front of them and rushed the burning wall. As the carpet fell against the fiery curtains, the window broke. Frank and Joe dragged the drapes down off the rods. The carpet fell over the mound of burning fabric. Shards from the broken window were scattered everywhere.

Frank began stomping the carpet with his feet to put out the rest of the flames just as Callie rushed into the room with a small fire extinguisher.

"This was in the hall downstairs," she said, pulling the pin and aiming the hose. Seconds later white foam blanketed the smoldering remains of the drapes and the scorched carpet, squelching the fire for good.

"Just like in the outline," Joe commented, surveying the charred material. "A mysterious fire in a locked room burns down the house."

"Except we know who set this fire," Callie pointed out.

Frank nodded. "Yeah. But where's Bev now?"

"She must have gone into the secret passageway," Joe said. He pointed to a wall that had the same paneling they'd seen in Callie's bedroom closet. It was composed of hundreds of small squares, all of them identical in size and color.

"Let me take a look," Frank said, examining the wall closely.

"I'll get Mr. Stevens," Callie volunteered. "He can show us how to open it." She sprinted from the room.

"Stevens said that every room has its own release," Joe said. He tried pressing against a few of the squares.

"I don't think the release is one of those squares," Frank said.

"Why not?"

"Because if it was part of the paneling, one of the squares would look different from the rest,"

Frank told him. "This is a game to Stevens. He likes to drop clues."

"The only other thing on the wall is the bookshelf," Joe said. He ran his hand over the volumes on the shelf. "They're all reference books. Dictionaries, a thesaurus." Joe tapped the gold-embossed binding of one book. *"The Arabian Nights' Entertainments,"* he read out loud.

"That's not a reference book. It's a book of short stories." Frank grinned with sudden understanding. "Including its most famous story—'Ali Baba and the Forty Thieves!' "

"Right," said Joe. "In which the secret door to the treasure cave is opened by saying 'Open Sesame.' " Joe tugged at the book. He felt some resistance at first, but then the volume pulled forward.

Joe heard a soft noise as a latch dropped. The paneling separated.

The back wall rolled open. Fixed to a metal rod, the *Arabian Nights* book pulled itself back into place.

Frank was stepping into the passageway when Callie called him back.

Flushed, Callie was leaning against the office entrance. "The—the window," she panted.

Joe looked through the broken glass. "It's Bev!" he cried out, watching a slim figure hurry across the front lawn. "She's heading for her car."

Joe dashed from the room with Frank right

behind him. One after the other they hurtled down the stairs. Throwing the front door open, Joe ran onto the covered porch.

At the far end of the curved driveway, Bev was climbing into her sports car. Joe charged toward the vehicle as she started its engine. Out of breath, he reached the car a second too late. Bev had the car in gear and was stepping on its accelerator.

With tires spinning, the car shot out from under Joe's outstretched hand. With Frank close behind him, Joe chased after it. He could hear Bev's laughter as the red two-seater sped away from him.

Just then Lipp's car appeared through the front gates of the property. "Stop her!" Joe shouted as he and Frank continued to run toward Bev's car.

Lipp braked sharply when he heard Joe. Slamming his luxury car into reverse, Lipp swung its long body across the exit.

Bev's escape was blocked. Downshifting, she spun her steering wheel and drove onto the lawn. She aimed the car toward the back of the property.

Joe and Frank skidded to a stop at Lipp's vehicle. The agent opened the car door and got out. "What's going on?"

"Long story," Joe said, catching his breath.

Frank watched as Bev's car bounced over the rough terrain of the back garden. A rear tire ran over an upended metal rake, sending it flying. "Where does she think she's going?" he asked.

"It doesn't matter," Joe responded. "She isn't going any farther." The sports car had stopped moving. Tilted to one side, it sat in a tangle of dead flowers.

Lipp and the Hardys walked back up the driveway. Callie and Mark had come out through the front door and stood to the side of the house to see what Bev would do.

"I've told Mr. Stevens everything," Callie said to Frank and Joe.

"My own secretary left the death threat?" Stevens said in a stricken voice. "And tried to burn down my house? How could she do this to me?"

Lipp was astounded by the news. "Bev is responsible for the things that have happened here?"

"For some of them, anyway," Frank replied. "We don't have all the answers yet."

"I need to sit down." Shakily, Lipp walked toward the mansion and lowered himself onto the front steps.

Stevens stayed with him. Frank, Joe, and Callie approached the red sports car that had flattened bushes and torn up the lawn.

As Frank and Joe got closer, they discovered why the car was tilted to one side—its rear tire was flat. "That's what you get for driving over a rake," Joe said.

Through the tinted glass of the windshield,

Frank could see that Bev was hunched over her car phone. She'd locked the car doors.

" . . . Nightmare House," Frank heard Bev say as she hung up the phone. Putting the receiver back, she glared at the Hardys defiantly.

"You might as well come out," Frank told her. "You're not going anywhere."

Bev turned away from him.

"Give it up, Frank," Joe said. "The police will get her out."

He started to turn away. When he did, Bev kicked the driver's door open, smashing it into Joe's backside. The blow sent him stumbling. Unable to stop himself, he bowled right into his brother.

The two of them tumbled to the ground in a tangle of arms and legs.

Bev bolted from the car. Pushing Callie aside, she ran for the back fence.

Callie took off after her. Joe sat up as Frank boosted himself to his feet.

"Come on!" Frank cried, joining the footrace across the estate lawn.

Joe chased after him. Bev was far ahead of them. She was almost at the fence when Callie threw herself forward, clutching for the other girl's waist. The two of them fell onto the grass.

Frank and Joe caught up with them as Callie stood up. Holding the struggling secretary by her arm, she pulled her upright.

"Let go of me!" Bev snapped.

"My pleasure," Callie said, releasing Bev's arm. Thrown off balance, Bev fell back to the ground.

Frank reached down for her. "We're taking you back to the house," he said.

Bev silently walked back to the mansion, her arms crossed in front of her.

As they neared the front porch, Joe caught Callie's attention. "Not bad," he said. "And you said you weren't any good at detective work."

"Thanks," she replied, pleased.

Stevens stood up as his secretary came up the steps. "How could you, Bev?" he asked, peering intently into her brown eyes. "How could you do any of those things?"

She didn't answer. Thrusting her chin out, she walked past him.

Lipp stood up. "You don't have to talk to us," he told her, "but you'll have to speak to the police. Arson is serious."

Bev paled. Michelle opened the front door, allowing everyone to enter the mansion.

Bev sat by herself on a sofa in the living room. Joe took a position by the front door while Frank guarded the entryway. The others found chairs to sit in.

Stevens called the police. They could all hear his end of the conversation. "I'd like a squad car sent to my address," he said. "No, no. It's not an emergency."

125

A short time later the doorbell rang. Michelle headed for the door, but Joe stopped her. "I'll get it," he said, opening the door.

Deke Ramsey was waiting in the opening. Joe stared at him, speechless.

"I want to speak to Bev Hart," Ramsey said.

Bev lifted her head. There were tears in her eyes.

Lipp rose from his chair. "I told you Ramsey was behind this, didn't I? They can share the same jail cell!"

"You lousy crook," Ramsey told him scornfully. "You can't prove anything. Sit down and shut up."

"I suppose you've come for your accomplice," Stevens said.

"No," Ramsey replied. "I've come to see my daughter."

Chapter

14

"YOUR DAUGHTER!" Joe exclaimed.

"That's right." Pushing Joe aside, Ramsey entered the house and went to the sofa to sit next to Bev. Taking his handkerchief, she wiped her eyes.

Bev then smoothed the handkerchief over her lap. She lowered her head and brought her right hand up to her eye. Something small and brown fell onto the handkerchief.

"It's a contact lens," Frank said, surprised. Bev's left eye was still brown. The other eye was slate gray—just like Ramsey's.

Looking at Bev, Frank was reminded of the photo in the bookstore—Ramsey's family picture. Bev didn't want anyone to notice the resemblance between her and her father, Frank thought. "You wore contacts as a disguise," Frank said.

Bev removed her second lens. "I've always hated these things!" she declared.

Ramsey patted her hand. "You don't have to wear them any longer."

"They've called the police, Dad," Bev said nervously.

"Hush," Ramsey said.

"They found the magazine," Bev told her father. "They know I left the threat on Stevens's desk."

"What about the mask that fell off the wall at the Ashfork Playhouse?" Joe demanded. "Are you responsible for that, too?"

Bev nodded sullenly. "When Lipp sent a note to Mr. Stevens explaining Joyce's publicity stunt with the mask, I intercepted it. And I arranged for my brother, Carl, to get the job installing it. He made sure it would fall down—"

"Hush," Ramsey repeated. "There's no proof about any of this!"

"She just confessed to it," Joe pointed out. "In front of witnesses."

Ramsey was obviously shaken by Joe's words.

"That's not all," Lipp spoke up. "Someone has been destroying Mark's private property. His garden, his mirrors, which were antiques and worth thousands of dollars. Not to mention setting fire to the house. I'm certain that the police will want to have a long talk with your daughter."

Sinking back against the sofa's cushions, Ramsey gave a long and weary sigh. "Leave Bev out of it," he told Stevens. "When the police come, I'll take responsibility for everything."

"Dad!" Bev cried.

"Is it a deal?" Ramsey asked Stevens.

"Maybe," Stevens replied. "I want to know the rest of it. What you did, and why you did it."

"You can't be serious, Mark," Lipp said. "You don't bargain with this sort of man. Let the police deal with him!"

"Well, Deke?" Stevens asked, ignoring Lipp.

"You know why," Ramsey said. "What are your other questions?"

Stevens drummed his fingers on the arm of his chair. "When are you going to stop, Deke?" he asked. "When will this vendetta be over?"

"Never," Ramsey spat. "Are all your questions going to be this easy?"

Stevens didn't answer.

"You followed the outline to frighten Mr. Stevens," Frank spoke up. "But how did Bev shatter the mirrors without waking anybody up?"

"It's okay," Ramsey told his daughter. "Tell him."

"It was easy," she answered with pride. "I did it on Michelle's night off, after Stevens had gone to sleep. I put a pillow on the mirrors and hit them with a hammer. Sometimes it took two or three hits, but it hardly made any noise at all.''

"What did you do to the flower garden?" Joe asked.

"I put weed killer in the fertilizer," she replied. "The more anyone tried to help the flowers, the worse they got." Triumph shone in her eyes.

"That was you in the secret passage behind Callie's room, wasn't it?" Frank demanded. "You were trying to frighten her, but you cut yourself on a nail and left a trail of blood for us to follow."

Again Bev nodded.

"We only meant to scare you," Ramsey said to Stevens. "We wanted to stop you from writing your novel. No one was supposed to get hurt."

"Broken mirrors and dead roses might not hurt anyone, but Joe could have been badly injured when you dropped that ax on him on the stairs," Michelle said. "Or when you tried to poison Mr. Lipp."

Inwardly Joe smiled. "I thought you said it was an accident," he told her.

"I've changed my mind," Michelle replied.

"I never touched Joe," Bev swore. "He *must* have tripped. And I certainly didn't try to poison anyone. Don't bother asking me about the tombstone, either, or the snakes in Stevens's office. I don't know anything about them." She was met with nothing but doubting faces. "I don't!" she insisted.

"What about the computer disks in my room?" Callie asked. "Do you know anything about those?"

"I put them there," Bev admitted. "I wanted you out of here."

"Bev told me about the tombstone," Ramsey said. "She didn't have anything to do with it." He coughed. "My son, Carl, is a headstrong boy. He does things without telling me. He could have been involved."

"Where is Carl?" Frank asked.

Ramsey gave him a dirty look. "He's moving things into our new apartment."

Uh-oh, Frank thought. The bookstore owner really must have been angry. She must have thrown them out.

"Carl is a bit hot-tempered," Ramsey said. "I thought it best that he remain at home."

"What about—" Joe's question was cut off by the door chimes.

"The police," Ramsey said, rising. "Don't forget our bargain. I'll do all the talking."

"I have more questions," Stevens said.

"We can talk at the police station." Ramsey offered his arm to Bev. "Come, my dear."

That night Michelle prepared a sumptuous meal to celebrate. "The nightmare is finally over," she said.

Stevens raised his glass of red wine to his guests. "To my three fabulous detectives," he toasted. "We couldn't have solved our mystery without them!"

"Here, here!" Lipp joined in, lifting his own glass.

Callie took a sip of water. "Ramsey ruined his entire life because of his desire for revenge," she said. "I can't help but feel a little sorry for him."

"I feel a certain responsibility myself," Lipp remarked.

"Why is that?" Frank asked.

"Years ago Deke Ramsey was my client," Lipp said. "I gave him an idea for a novel—it became his fourth book—and he promised to pay me for it. He never did."

"Shouldn't you be the one wanting revenge?" Joe asked.

"You're right." Lipp smiled. "Instead, I quit. When I did, I took my other idea for a book with me. I asked Mark to turn it into a novel."

"Colors of the Dead," Stevens said. "The only idea of Robert's that I ever used. Don't worry—I paid him for it."

A pained expression crossed Lipp's face. "Deke decided that that story line was his. Of course, he never said a word until Mark's book was a hit." He drained his glass. "Ramsey had never been very stable, and I worry that my leaving him might have pushed him over the edge.

If I hadn't worked with Ramsey, he may not have gone after Mark.''

"How did Bev get involved with all of this?" Frank wanted to know.

"The police told me that after his divorce, Ramsey stayed in contact with his kids," Stevens explained. "In his letters he told them that I'd stolen his big idea. Apparently, they believed him."

"So they decided to get back at you, right?" Joe said. "They decided to steal your next story idea—and give it to their father."

"Exactly," the writer agreed. "And they tried to frighten me into abandoning my book."

Frank poked at his food. Everything made sense—to a point. Something was missing, though.

"What did Ramsey say about Bad Mac McCoy?" Joe asked.

"According to the police, Deke hadn't heard of him," Stevens replied. "Neither had Bev."

"If they were telling the truth," Lipp said pointedly. "His son, Carl, was probably behind it."

"In any case, it's over," Stevens said. "Now there's nothing to keep me from finishing my manuscript." He brightened as Michelle came into the room, carrying a silver platter with a huge cheesecake on it. "Ah, dessert!"

It was nearly midnight when the last of the dishes were cleared away. "I think I'll get some air," Lipp said, excusing himself. "It's a nice night for a drive."

"It's past my bedtime," Mark announced. "I'll see all of you in the morning."

Frank, Joe, and Callie climbed the stairs to the second floor. Joe went to his room, letting Frank walk Callie to her door.

A few minutes later Frank wandered back into their room. "What's that?" Joe asked, nodding at the folder in Frank's hand.

"The file on Stevens's first book" he said. "We left it in Callie's room, remember? I promised to return it."

"Meanwhile, you might want to take a look at it."

"I might," Frank admitted. Tossing it on the nightstand, he dropped down to his bed. Folding his hands behind his head, he stared up at the ceiling.

"I know that look," Joe said. "You're thinking again. What's the matter?"

"Nothing," Frank replied. He sat up, swinging his legs off the bed. "No, that's not true. Something isn't right about this case. I can feel it."

"Like what?" Joe asked.

Frank grinned sheepishly. "I'm not sure."

Joe shook his head. "Good night, Frank. Maybe you should sleep on it." He reached for the lamp on the nightstand, and turned it off.

Frank got ready for bed. Once under the covers, he still couldn't sleep. A thousand thoughts raced through his brain.

"I give up." Rolling onto his side, Frank turned on the light by the bed. Joe slept peacefully, undisturbed.

Frank grabbed the folder from the nightstand. It didn't matter, now, who'd had the idea first for the novel. Still, it gave him something to do—and he wanted to know the answer.

He opened the folder, sending loose pages fluttering to the bed. Frank frowned. He hadn't remembered seeing quite so many notes before.

"A sure cure for insomnia," he muttered. Propping himself up on his pillow, he began to scan the pages. If Robert Lipp had put the idea on paper, it had to be in there somewhere.

Minutes later Frank found it. There were eight typewritten pages, paper-clipped together. Lipp had penned a short message on the front page, asking Stevens to give the idea his consideration.

No wonder Lipp wanted to be paid for this, Frank thought. He'd provided the entire story line for a novel, start to finish. It was well-written, too.

Almost too well-written.

Frank pulled Lipp's other letters, checking to see if their writing style matched that of the outline. He couldn't tell. Everything else concerned business matters. The letters were full of stilted language and legal jargon.

He gazed at the outline, concerned. There was no way to tell if Lipp had written it. No date appeared on the pages—

Frank's jaw dropped open. He twisted the head of his lamp, shining its light directly on the outline.

"I don't believe it," he told himself.

Climbing out of bed, he opened the nightstand drawer. He took out a folded sheet of paper and compared it to the outline.

They were a match.

He jostled Joe's shoulder. "Wake up."

"What?" Joe mumbled.

"You've got to get up," Frank said urgently. "There's trouble. Big trouble!"

Chapter

15

JOE KICKED off his covers. "What are you talking about?"

"Something's been bothering me," Frank said. "Ever since Ramsey was arrested, I've had the feeling that this case wasn't over, that it still had loose ends." He gave Joe the sheet of paper that he'd taken from the nightstand drawer. "This is one of them."

It was the piece of stationery that Frank had brought back from Ashfork Granite and Marble. Joe glanced at it and shrugged. "It's the tombstone letter."

"Take a better look," Frank said. "The monument company used it like an order form. After they filled the order, they stamped it."

The stationery's upper right-hand corner was

stamped Paid in red ink. Below the stamp someone had written Grave Marker and the purchase
price.

Joe raised an eyebrow at the price.
"Expensive."

"Too expensive for the Ramseys," Frank remarked. He laid Lipp's story line beside the
piece of stationery. "Compare the two."

"They're both from a manual typewriter—the
same typewriter," Joe said. The battered lowercase *s* couldn't be missed.

He looked at Lipp's note on the front page of
the story line, then shook his head in confusion.
"You think Robert Lipp ordered the tombstone?"

"He's got the money for it," Frank replied.

"True enough," Joe said, remembering the
agent's sleek luxury car. "He also has the
money to hire somebody like Bad Mac McCoy.
But Bev already confessed."

"She confessed to the little things," Frank
said. "The ones she could do herself. I think it
was Bev's idea to scare Stevens by following his
outline. Lipp must have heard about all that was
happening and decided to do it, too."

Joe thought about it. "The timing's right," he
admitted. "If Stevens was too frightened to
write, he'd have called his agent."

"And that would have brought Lipp out to the
mansion," Frank put in. "While he pretended to

encourage his client's writing, he was really trying to stop him. Now, if we only knew why."

Moving to their bedroom window, Joe looked down. "Lipp's car isn't in the driveway."

"He must really enjoy the night air," Frank said dryly. "He's been gone a long time."

"As long as Lipp's out of the house," Joe said, "let's search his bedroom. We won't get another chance like this."

Frank nodded.

Frank and Joe dressed quickly and went out into the hall. Once Frank's eyes adjusted to the darkness, he led the way to Lipp's room. He pushed the door open.

There was a blanket folded on top of Lipp's bed. Frank hung it over the curtain rod. "That ought to keep the light in. If Lipp comes back, he won't see that we're in his room."

Joe clicked on the table lamp. "Let's get to work."

Frank went over the room while Joe searched through the closet. They worked in silence, each intent on his task.

"Any luck?" Joe finally asked.

"Only this," Frank replied, holding up a silver key. "It was taped to the bottom of the nightstand drawer. But it doesn't fit anything."

"Wanna bet?" Joe lifted up a black leather briefcase. "This was in the back of the closet—and it's locked."

Frank handed him the key, and Joe slid it into

the lock. Raising the briefcase's lid, he found a single notebook inside. "It felt heavier," he said, disappointed.

Frank opened the notebook. "It's an accounting ledger. It lists how much money Stevens has made on his books." Each page indicated the royalties that had been received on a particular novel.

Joe didn't respond. He was holding the briefcase sideways, peering down its surface.

"What are you doing?" Frank asked.

Joe displayed the empty briefcase. "It *still* feels like there's something in here," he insisted. Laying the case on his lap, he ran his fingers over the lid's interior lining.

"Found it," he murmured. Joe tugged at a corner of the lining. Frank heard a snapping noise, and then the lining suddenly pulled free.

A false bottom popped open, and a second ledger slid out of its hiding place onto Joe's lap.

Joe opened the new ledger. Like the first, it contained a listing of Stevens's royalties. He compared it against the book that Frank held. "The numbers don't match," Joe said.

Frank peeked over Joe's shoulder. "This explains why Lipp has two sets of accounting books," he said.

"Yeah," Joe agreed. "He's been embezzling from Stevens!"

Standing by the window, Frank heard the

sound of a car approaching. Someone was coming up the driveway. "The lights," Frank hissed.

Quickly shifting the briefcase off his lap, Joe found the table lamp. He switched it off, and the room went black.

The engine noise swung away from the bedroom, going farther down the driveway. Then the sound stopped.

A moment later a car door opened and closed. After that, Frank heard the closing of a second car door.

Two doors? he thought. Pushing back the blanket, Frank peered outside.

The outside grounds were lit by bright moonlight. Lipp's car was a distance away, parked at the far side of the driveway. The luxury car was empty.

"He must be going to the back door," Frank said. "We'd better hurry."

Joe turned on the lamp. He laid aside the second ledger and snapped the briefcase's interior lining into place. "We'll keep the second notebook for evidence," Joe said. "I'll put the briefcase back."

While Joe returned the briefcase to the closet, Frank refolded the blanket, leaving it on the bed. He turned off the light, and they slipped out of the bedroom.

Back in their own room, Joe hid the ledger behind the nightstand. Frank stayed at the door, watching for Lipp's arrival.

After several minutes, Frank said, "No sign of him. He must have stayed downstairs."

"Why would he do that?" Joe asked.

"I don't know," Frank said, "but I think we'd better find out."

They tiptoed down the stairs, stopping at the bottom of the landing.

"This way," Joe whispered, pointing to a light shining at the back of the house. Using the walls to guide him, Joe moved toward it.

As he neared the basement door, he saw light streaming out from under it. Reaching for the doorknob, Joe slowly pulled it forward.

The hinges squeaked. Joe paused, listening for any noise from below.

There was a shuffling sound from inside the basement. "Who's there?" a voice demanded.

Joe opened the door the rest of the way. Robert Lipp was at the bottom of the basement steps, peering up at them.

"Joe, Frank," he said weakly. "You shouldn't sneak around like that."

"Sorry," Joe said.

"It's okay. I was surprised, that's all." Lipp took a step forward, climbing toward them. "What are you doing down here?"

"We were going to the kitchen for a snack," Joe improvised smoothly. "We saw a light on."

"You wanted some of Michelle's cheesecake,

am I right?'' Lipp wet his lips anxiously. ''Well, don't let me keep you from it.''

He stayed in the center of the stairs, watching them with bright eyes.

Lipp's hiding something, Frank thought. He's blocking the steps to stop us from going down to the basement.

''Why are you still up?'' Joe asked.

''I couldn't sleep,'' Lipp confessed. ''It's a problem that affects us old men.''

''I thought you used a sedative,'' Joe said.

''Umm—yes,'' he said, faltering. ''Most nights I do.''

Lipp continued to block the stairs. Oh, no, you don't, Frank thought. You're not stopping me that easily.

He made his move. Pushing the agent aside, Frank bounded down the steps.

Once off the stairs, he had a clear view of the torture chamber. Frank looked past Stevens's toys, trying to see some sign that another person was in the basement.

There wasn't anyone else there. Frank felt his face grow hot with embarrassment.

''What do you think you're doing?'' Lipp snapped, folding his arms.

''Oh, boy,'' Frank muttered. ''I thought . . .''

''Yes?''

''Nothing,'' Frank concluded lamely. He faced the smaller man. ''I made a mistake.''

''I guess you did,'' Lipp said coldly. ''You

boys better go to the kitchen and get your snack. I'll lock up down here.''

Lipp let his arms drop. When he did, Frank noticed that his right palm had left a dark smear on the sleeve of his jacket.

It looked like a streak of grease. Frank moved back toward the torture chamber.

What was Lipp doing down here? Frank thought. There wasn't much in the basement, except for Stevens's toys.

Frank walked back toward the machines.

Joe started down the stairs. "What is it, Frank?"

Lipp held out a hand to stop Joe. "I want both of you out of here!" he said shrilly.

Frank kept walking. As he neared the guillotine, he saw that its release lever had been tripped. Its sharp blade was at the base of the unit, below the point where someone would rest his or her neck. Frank drew his breath in sharply.

Instantly he knew what it meant. Lipp had removed the safety catch! The next time Stevens played his little prank with the guillotine, there would be nothing to stop the blade from falling.

It wasn't a toy any longer. Now it was all too real.

Knocking Lipp's arm back, Joe came onto the basement floor. "Frank?"

Frank shook his head. "Tell you later.''

"Why wait?" Lipp asked. Turning, they saw that he'd followed Joe down the stairs.

Lipp looked from Frank to the guillotine. "I see you've discovered my handiwork," he said. "You're very clever. Too clever for your own good, perhaps."

What's he talking about?" Joe asked. Frank gestured toward the guillotine.

Joe's eyes widened.

"My bright young detectives," Lipp said, shaking his head. "Mac!" he called.

"Here," a voice replied. Bad Mac McCoy stepped out from under the dark recesses of the open stairwell.

He folded one of his big hands shut, curling his fingers into an oversize fist. "What do you want me to do with them?" McCoy asked.

"I'm afraid we have no choice," Lipp said. "We'll have to kill them."

Chapter

16

FRANK FELT his muscles tense. Joe raised his fists, ready to fight.

McCoy wasn't paying any attention to them. He stared at the agent, a confused look on his face. "*Kill* them?"

"We have no other choice," Lipp responded. "They've seen too much." He slipped his hand inside his jacket and pulled out a silver automatic.

Frank took a step forward, and Lipp brought the gun up sharply. "Get back," he said.

McCoy nervously wiped a hand across his forehead. He's not as bloodthirsty as he looks, Joe thought.

"I don't want any part of this," the body-builder said. "I've done a lot of your dirty work, but if you want a murderer, you'll have to get a different man."

"You disappoint me, Mac," Lipp said. "I thought you had a reputation."

"I hurt people," McCoy replied. "I don't kill them!"

"You're only good for tombstones and snakes, is that it? I feared as much." Lipp leveled the gun at him. "Move over, McCoy. I want the three of you together."

McCoy obeyed, walking slowly over to the Hardys.

From the rear wall there came the sound of a latch being lifted. "Keep still," Lipp said.

"And if we don't?" Joe asked.

Lipp's finger curled around the trigger of the gun. "That would be a mistake."

He backed up to the stairway, his weapon trained on his captives. Frank and Joe knew that anyone coming out of the secret corridor would not be able to see Lipp.

The basement wall slid open. Callie gave Frank a relieved smile as she stepped into the room. Mark Stevens was right behind her.

"Callie," Frank said as a warning.

Her eyes took in the muscular giant standing between Frank and Joe, and a line creased her brow.

Stevens frowned at the unexpected visitor. "Callie's been looking for you," he said to the Hardys. "When she found your room was empty, she woke me up. I suggested we check the passageway."

Lipp had turned his head toward the newcomers. Catching Callie's eye, Frank risked giving a tiny nod toward the open tunnel.

Callie saw it. "Let's go back," she urged Stevens in a low voice.

"Don't be ridiculous," Stevens said. "I want to know what's going on in here."

Lipp moved into their sight lines. "Let me answer that," he said. He aimed his automatic at Callie. "Don't leave us, Miss Shaw."

She stiffened at the sight of the gun.

For the moment Lipp's attention was focused fully on Callie. Still, Frank knew that he didn't dare rush him. Someone would get hurt.

Frank could see that Joe had an idea of his own. Moving cautiously, his younger brother was edging away from Bad Mac McCoy.

"Robert?" Stevens started toward the agent. "What's going on?"

Lipp swung the gun around. "Stand with the others."

"I don't understand." Dumbfounded, Stevens remained in place.

"Moron!" Lipp spat. "I told you to move." He gave a half turn, waving his weapon in the direction of the Hardys.

His gun hand froze in midair. "Where is Joe Hardy?" Lipp thundered.

His question went unanswered. Lipp's expression told Frank that Joe's disappearing act had worked. Frank and McCoy were backed up against the wooden frame of the rack. To their left was the guillotine, to their right, the iron maiden.

Lipp advanced on Frank. "Where did he go?"

"Who?" Frank countered blandly.

"Don't play games with me." Lipp raised his gun, pressing it to Frank's head. "Where is your brother?"

Frank swallowed. "He had to step out," he said.

Lipp's eyes narrowed. "I imagine you think you're being brave." He glanced over at McCoy. "You're not brave, are you, Mac?"

He turned the automatic on the bodybuilder. McCoy looked as if he was ready to faint.

"Tell me where Joe went," Lipp commanded.

McCoy was too frightened to speak. His eyes flicked over to the iron maiden.

The large woman-shaped box was only a few feet from where Joe had been standing. Made of black metal, the iron maiden stood upright on its base. Eight feet tall and over three feet wide, it looked like an oversize casket.

A casket's interior isn't lined with spikes, Frank thought, but the iron maiden is. Anyone trapped inside it would die a grisly death, impaled on long, sharp stakes.

Frank saw a smile cross Lipp's face when he noticed that the iron maiden's door was still ajar.

"Foolish lad," Lipp said. "You should have chosen a better hiding place." Striding over to the big box, he placed his hand against the door.

"Don't close it!" Callie cried. "You'll kill him!"

"What a shame." Lipp slammed the door shut.

Frank winced as it banged hollowly, closing on an empty chamber.

Hiding behind the iron maiden, Joe kicked out with his leg. Lipp jumped aside as the metal cage crashed downward.

Wailing in terror, Stevens turned and ran. He thudded into the secret passageway, his retreating footsteps echoing from inside.

Lipp spun around, his gun in front of him, and aimed it at Stevens.

Frank was already moving and leapt for the gun as Lipp fired.

He was too late. Struck from behind, Stevens cried out. The writer crumpled, falling to the ground.

Lipp's victory was short-lived. Pulling away from Frank, he clutched at his chest. With his face twisted in pain, he slumped to the floor with what Frank guessed was a heart attack.

"Call an ambulance!" Joe cried out to Callie. "We'll try CPR on Lipp."

A few days later Frank, Joe, and Callie went to visit Stevens in the hospital. On their way into his room they were met by Joyce Halloran, his publicist.

"My phone's been ringing off the hook!" she exclaimed happily. "Every TV news show and newspaper in the country wants to do a feature on Mark Stevens."

"Did you ever speak with Tim, the reporter from the *Gazette?*" Joe asked.

"He got an exclusive," Joyce said. "It was just what he wanted—a big front-page piece."

Giving them a wide smile, she bustled on down the hospital corridor.

Stevens was sitting up in bed as they entered. "My heroes," he said in a bright voice. "I was hoping you'd come by."

"How's the arm?" Joe asked.

"Sore," he answered. Taped and immobile, his left arm lay across his chest. "But the doctors say it'll be fine. I'll be back writing in no time."

"We saw a police guard stationed at the end of the hallway," Callie commented.

"That's Robert Lipp's room," Stevens said. "He'll be moved once his condition improves."

Frank felt relieved. "He's going to live, then."

"It was close," the writer said. "If you two hadn't administered CPR, Lipp almost certainly would have died. He thought he was going to, so he made a deathbed confession."

"Did he say why he tried to kill you?" Joe wondered.

"Yes, he did," the writer replied grimly. "As you suspected, he'd been embezzling from me. My royalty checks were sent to his office, and I trusted him to deposit them for me. I guess the temptation got to be too much. Lipp started stealing from me."

"How long was this going on?" Callie asked.

"For years," Stevens replied. "But Lipp knew it couldn't continue. He was sick and desperately needed to retire. I'd insisted on it."

"He was stuck, wasn't he?" Frank said. "He couldn't retire. Because if he did, a new agent might spot the discrepancies in your account."

"Right."

"What was the purpose of the snakes and the tombstone?" Joe asked.

"Don't forget Joe's fall down the stairs," Callie added.

"Like Bev, Lipp wanted to frighten me into abandoning my new novel," Stevens explained. "He knew it would take me months to start another project—and he'd be able to remain my agent until I did. He'd use the extra time to disappear quietly."

"With your money," Frank said.

"With a chunk of it, anyway." Stevens shifted in his bed. "But things didn't go the way Lipp planned. Having you guys around to protect me, I'd stopped being quite so scared. I started writing again. Once Ramsey was caught, I told everyone that I was going to finish my book."

Stevens sighed. "Lipp couldn't let that happen—so he planned to kill me."

"With the guillotine," Joe said.

"Right. He was going to make it appear that one of my tricks had backfired on me."

"What about the poisoned water that Lipp drank?" Frank asked.

"Apparently there was no poison," Stevens said. "He faked it—and made sure the pitcher was smashed when he pretended to collapse so the water couldn't be analyzed. It was just another scare tactic that imitated the outline of my novel."

"He might have succeeded, if the three of you hadn't stopped him," Michelle said. She had quietly slipped into the room behind them.

Stevens clasped her hand. "I haven't had much luck with my employees, but this one's a gem."

Michelle blushed prettily.

"One last question," Joe said. "Was Deke Ramsey right? Did Lipp steal Deke's outline for *Colors of the Dead?*"

"I haven't wanted to admit it to myself," Stevens told him, "but, yes, I think he did."

"What's going to happen to Ramsey?" Callie asked.

"Better things, I hope. I've dropped the charges against him, and I'll be meeting with him in a week or so. I'll try to make things right." Stevens leaned back against his pillow. "One thing's for sure. Deke won't need to work in a bookstore any longer."

After a few minutes of conversation, the three friends left the hospital. Opening the driver's door of the van, Joe asked, "What do you want to do now?"

"We could see a movie," Callie suggested. With a sparkle in her eye she added, "There's a new horror picture playing at the mall."

Frank and Joe both groaned.

"No more horror pictures for me," Frank said. "They can't begin to compare with real life."

Frank and Joe's next case:

The Hardy boys have come to Chicago with their father to attend a meeting of computer experts at the Evanco building. But suddenly, without warning, the 120-story skyscraper is turned into a tower of terror. A gang of gunmen invades the offices, snatches an attractive young college woman, and disappears into the night!

Her name is Sarah Evans, daughter of the rich and reclusive owner of Evanco, J. P. Evans, and her kidnapping is the key to a global conspiracy of computer destruction. The world's most powerful computers have been turned into long-distance time bombs, and Frank and Joe are racing the clock both to save Sarah and defuse the ultimate high-tech weapon . . . in *Screamers*, Case #72 in The Hardy Boys Casefiles™.